'I think our government needs the help of some outside force to survive as a democracy.' The President of the United States looked up ...

'You, Dr. Smith, will head that outside force. Your assignment will be to work outside the constitution to preserve the process of this government. Where there is corruption, end it. Where there is crime, stop it. Use any means you wish ... Help me protect our nation Dr. Smith.'

This was the creation of the organisation known as CURE: the final alternative when the machinery of security failed; the agency that exists for only four people—the President of the United States, Dr. Harold Smith, Chiun—an ancient Korean who learned how to kill from the age of eighteen months—and Remo Williams—the man they resurrected from the electric chair and programmed to destroy ...

Also by Richard Sapir and Warren Murphy

CREATED, THE DESTROYER
THE DESTROYER: CHINESE PUZZLE
THE DESTROYER: DEATH CHECK
THE DESTROYER: MAFIA FIX
THE DESTROYER: DR. QUAKE
THE DESTROYER: DEATH THERAPY

and published by Corgi Books

The Destroyer: Union Bust

Richard Sapir and Warren Murphy

CORGI BOOKS
A DIVISION OF TRANSWORLD PUBLISHERS LTD

THE DESTROYER: UNION BUST

A CORGI BOOK 0 552 09636 9

First publication in Great Britain 1974

PRINTING HISTORY

Corgi edition published 1974

This book is set in Baskerville 10/11 pt.

Corgi Books are published by Transworld Publishers Ltd., Cavendish House, 57–59 Uxbridge Road, Ealing, London, W.5.

Made and printed in Great Britain by Richard Clay (The Chaucer Press), Ltd., Bungay, Suffolk.

NOTE: The Australian price appearing on the back cover is the recommended retail price.

For: Dan, Fred, Richard—
and especially Mimi,
who knows where
the Cow Palace
isn't.

ONE

What were they going to do, kill him?

Jimmy McQuade had worked his installer crew to the limit, and he wasn't going to work them one more hour, not if the district supervisor got on his knees and begged, not if the president of the International Communication Workers threatened to kick him out of the union, not if they raised the double overtime to triple overtime like last week, during Easter.

His crew was falling asleep at the job. A half hour before, one of his senior linemen working outside made a mistake a rookie wouldn't think of, and now the old man assembling one of the gaggle of WATS lines connections had passed out.

'Okay. Everybody off the job,' said Jimmy McQuade, shop steward of Local 283 International Communications Workers, Chicago, Illinois.

'Go home and sleep. I don't want to see any of you for two days. This overtime pay isn't going to do dead men any good.'

Heads lifted. One young man kept working on his knees.

'We're going home. We're going to rest. Somebody shake the kid,' said Jimmy McQuade.

A gray-haired worker, telephone cords strung around his neck like leis, patted the youngster on the back.

'We're going to rest.'

The young man looked up, dazed.

'Yeah. Rest. Beautiful, baby. I forgot what it was like.'

He curled over his installer's box on his tool holster side and snored away in bliss.

'Leave him. Nobody's going to wake him,' said Jimmy McQuade.

'It's about time,' said an installer dropping his tools at his feet and making his way across the stacked beams and sacks of concrete to a bucket the men used to relieve themselves.

The plumbing had been installed, but so rapidly and by so few men that the toilets did not work. Some of the plaster was falling and it was only a day old.

The management had brought in carpenters to repair that by putting up plaster board. The plasterers did not object. Some of the men, Jimmy McQuade knew, had objected to the local president of the Plasterers' Union. What they got were little envelopes that paid them for the time they would not be working. Like typesetters in newspapers when advertisers brought in pre-set ads.

The difference was that the plasterers had nothing in their contracts stipulating such payment. But that was the plasterers. Jimmy McQuade was communications and he had worked at his job for twenty-four years and had been a good installer, a good supervisor, and a good union man. Supervisors were rarely made stewards. But the men trusted Jimmy McQuade so much that they insisted a rule of Local 283 be altered to allow him to hold both posts.

The amendment passed unanimously. He had to leave the union hall quickly because he didn't want anyone to see him cry. It was a good job until this building.

All the trade unions involved were secretly griping about it, he knew. Which was strange because there was more money coming in on this job than anyone could remember. Some of the electricians bought second homes on this job alone. It was the overtime. Some rich lunatic had decided a ten-story building would go up in two months. From scratch.

And if that wasn't weird enough, the telephone system

they wanted would have been ample for the Strategic Air Command headquarters. Jimmy knew a couple of men who had worked on that one. They had been screened as if they were going to personally get the plans to the hydrogen bomb.

Jimmy McQuade had been screened for this job. That should have warned him. He should have known there would be something screwy, that just maybe he would find himself not a shop steward or a crew supervisor but a slave driver working men sixteen-hour days nonstop for two weeks to meet the district supervisor's order:

'We don't care what else isn't ready. They want the phones. And they're going to get them. The phones have to be in and operating by April 17. I don't care what expenses, what delays you have. April 17.'

That was management. You could expect that sort of excitability from management. What was surprising was that the union was worse. It had started at the screening.

Jimmy McQuade had not known it was a screening. He had been invited by the international vice-president himself to union headquarters in Washington. The union would pick up his lost time. He had thought at first he was going to be appointed to some national labor post.

'I guess you want to know why I asked you here,' said the international vice-president. He sat behind a desk remarkably like the one used by the vice-president of the phone company. Although here the window opened to the Washington Monument instead of Lake Michigan.

'No,' said Jimmy smiling. 'I thought we'd play pinochle until the summer, then maybe go golfing until the fall.'

'Heh, heh, heh,' laughed the vice-president. He didn't sound as if his mirth were real. 'McQuade. How good a union man are you?'

'I'm a shop steward.'

'I mean how good?'

'Good.'

'Do you love your union?'

'Yeah. I guess so.'

'You guess so. If it were a choice between the union or going to jail, would you go to jail? Think about it.'

'You mean if someone were trying to break the union?'

'Right.'

Jimmy McQuade thought a moment. 'Yes,' he said. 'I'd go to jail.'

'Do you think union business is anybody else's business?'

'Well, not if we're not doing anything illegal.'

'I'm talking about giving information about union business to people outside the union.'

'Hell, no!'

'Even if they're some kind of cops?'

'Yeah. Even if they're some kind of cops.'

'You're a good union man. You've got a good union record and a good work record. There's a job starting that's important to all good union men. I can't tell you why, but it's important. And we don't want to go advertising it around.'

Jimmy McQuade nodded.

'I want you to select a fifteen-man crew of good union men, good workers who can keep their mouths shut. It's a job that would call for more than fifteen men, but that's the minimum, absolute minimum for completing this job in time. We don't want to be using any more people than we have to. If we had time, I'd do the damned thing myself. But we don't have time. Remember. Men who can work and keep quiet. There will be plenty of overtime.'

The vice-president reached into his large desk and brought out two envelopes. He held forth the fatter one.

'This is for you. I find it good policy never to let anyone else know what I'm making. It will serve you well to follow it. There may be a lot of pressure in this job, and what may be a small friction at the beginning, becomes a bigger one later on. This smaller one is for the men. Don't take it out of the envelope in front of them. Individually, personally on the side.'

The vice-president handed Jimmy McQuade the smaller envelope.

'It'll take me about two weeks to get the right crew,' said Jimmy McQuade.

The vice-president looked at his watch. 'We got you for departure from Dulles in forty minutes. Maybe you can make some phone calls from the airport. You can also make a few from the plane.'

'You can't phone from an airplane, a commercial liner.'

'That should be your biggest worry. Believe me, on that flight the pilot will give you anything you want. Take a stewardess, too, if it won't tire you out. You begin tonight. It's a small suburb outside of Chicago. Nuihc Street. That's it. Funny name. It's a new street, named by the builders. Actually it's just an access road now. For the bulldozers and things.'

The vice-president rose to shake Jimmy McQuade's hand.

'Good luck. We're counting on you. And when you're through, there's more than just that envelope. What the hell are you doing with those envelopes?'

Jimmy looked at the envelopes, puzzled.

'Don't walk out of here holding them in your hand. Put them in your pocket.'

'Oh, yeah,' said Jimmy McQuade. 'Look, I'm working at another building and the company....'

'That's been squared. That's been squared. Get out of here. You're going to miss your plane.'

Jimmy McQuade had opened the envelopes in the cab taking him to the airport. There was $3,500 for him, and $1,500 for the men. He decided to switch envelopes and give the men the $3,500, keeping the $1,500 for himself. This resolution kept wavering all the way to the airport, descending on the men's side, ascending on his until he was back to the original split.

He sat in first class and ordered a drink. He wasn't going to ask the stewardess to let him make a phone call from the plane. He would sound like an idiot asking that.

Halfway through his rye and ginger, the pilot came down the aisle.

'McQuade?'

'Yes.'

'Why the hell are you sitting here? We got the linkup to ground telephone.'

'Oh. Yeah,' said Jimmy McQuade. 'I just wanted to finish my drink.'

'You're wasting a fortune in time. Take the drink with you.'

'Into the cockpit?'

'Yes. C'mon. Wait. You're right.'

'I thought so. Federal Aeronautics Authority rules.'

'The stewardess will bring it. No point unsettling the passengers.'

When the surprised telephone crew reached Nuihc Street at two in the morning, they found only steel beams and men working under floodlights.

Jimmy McQuade looked for the builder. He found him guzzling coffee, yelling at a crane operator.

'I can't see the fuckin' roof. How the hell am I going to set it right?' yelled the operator.

'We'll get a flood up there. We'll get a flood,' the builder yelled back. He turned to Jimmy McQuade. 'Yeah. What do you want?'

'We're the phone installers. It looks like we're four months early.'

'No. You're late.'

'Where do you want the interoffice lines, in the cement?'

'Well, do what you can now. You have the plans. You could be stringing outside wire.'

'Most of my men are inside.'

'So work 'em outside. What's the big deal?'

'You don't know too much about phones, do you?'

'I know they're going to be working by April 17, is what I know.'

That was the first complaint. The president of the local said it wasn't up to him. Call the vice-president. The vice-president told Jimmy McQuade he didn't receive the money because it was an easy job.

Two weeks later, one of the inside men threatened to quit. More money came for Jimmy McQuade from Washington. When the other installers found out about this episode, they all threatened to quit. They all got more money.

Then one of the men did quit. Jimmy McQuade ran after him down Nuihc Street, now paved to a three-lane-wide thoroughfare. The man wouldn't listen. Jimmy McQuade phoned the vice-president of the union and asked if he could recruit another man to fill the crew.

'What was his name?' asked the vice-president.

'Johnny Delano,' said Jimmy McQuade. But he did not get another man. Nor did the quitter return.

And when the lineman committed the mistake of a rookie and the installer passed out, Jimmy McQuade had had it. Enough.

The kid slept over his tool box, and all the others filed into the new elevators, which they hoped would work this time. Jimmy McQuade went with his men.

He went home to his wife who had not known his body since he started the job. She embraced him passionately, shooed the kids off to bed, and undressed him. She took great care in the shower, and put on the special perfume he loved.

When she entered the bedroom, her husband was dead asleep. No matter. She knew what would wake him. She nibbled at his ear and ran a hand down his stomach to his navel.

All she got was a snore.

So Mrs. McQuade accidentally spilled a glass of water on her husband's face. He slept with a wet face.

At 3 A.M. there was a buzz at the door. Mrs. McQuade nudged her husband to answer it. He slept on.

She donned a bathrobe, and mumbling curses about

her husband's job, answered the door.

'FBI,' said one of two men, holding forth indentification. 'May we speak to your husband? We're awfully sorry to disturb you at this hour. But it's urgent.'

'I can't wake him,' said Mrs. McQuade.

'It's urgent,' said the spokesman of the pair.

'Yeah, well lots of things are urgent. I didn't say I wouldn't wake him, I said I couldn't.'

'Something wrong?'

'He's dead tired. He's been working without any really good sleep for almost two months.'

'We'd like to talk to him about that.'

Mrs. McQuade looked up and down the street to make sure no neighbors were watching, and reassured that at 3 A.M. this was highly unlikely, she invited the two agents into the house.

'He won't wake up,' said Mrs. McQuade, leading them to the bedroom. They waited at the bedroom door.

'He won't wake up,' she said again, and shook her husband's shoulder.

'Wha?' said Jimmy McQuade, opening his eyes.

'For this he wakes up,' said Mrs. McQuade. 'It's the FBI. They want to talk to you about overtime.'

'Tell them to do all the work they can outside if inside isn't ready yet.'

'The FBI.'

'Well, ask one of the older men. Do what you can. We can order any special parts we need.'

'The FBI has come to put you in jail for the rest of your life.'

'Yeah. Good. Do it.' said Jimmy McQuade and went off into his comfortable dark world.

'See,' said Mrs. McQuade with a strange sense of relief.

'Could you shake him again?' asked the spokesman for the pair.

Mrs. McQuade grabbed the closest piece of her husband and squeezed.

'Yeah. OK. Back to work,' said Jimmy McQuade bounding from bed. He looked around, saw two men without tools in their hands, and finding nothing in the room that needed connecting, suddenly realized he was not at the building site.

'Home. Yeah. Hello, honey. What are these men doing here?'

'We're from the FBI, Mr. McQuade, we'd like to talk to you.'

'Oh,' said Jimmy McQuade. 'Well. Okay.'

His wife made a big pot of coffee. They talked in the kitchen.

'Some pretty interesting things are going on at your new job aren't they?'

'It's a job,' said Jimmy McQuade.

'We believe it's more than a job. And we'd like your help.'

'Look. I'm a good citizen but I'm a union man, too.'

'Was Johnny Delano a union man also?'

'Yeah.'

'Was he a good union man.'

'Yeah.'

'Was he a good union man when he quit?'

'Yeah. He couldn't take it and walked off the job. But he's a good union man.'

The spokesman of the pair nodded and put a candid-size glossy photograph on the white formica of the kitchen table.

Jimmy McQuade looked at it.

'So. You got a picture of a pile of mud.'

'The pile's name is Johnny Delano,' said the FBI man.

Jimmy McQuade looked closer. 'Oh, no,' groaned Jimmy McQuade.

'They were able to identify him because there was a finger left. All the teeth had been crushed. Often we can identify someone through bridgework. But Johnny Delano's teeth were crushed. The body was dissolved and crushed at the same time. Police lab still can't figure it out. Neither can we. We don't know what did this to him. One finger was left intact. You see that thing protruding from the pile. It looks like a bump.'

'Okay. Okay. Okay. Stop. I got the general drift. What do you want? And put that picture back in your pocket.'

'I'd like to stress that we're not in union busting. It's just that your union is providing something that is going to hurt your members. We're also not in the union business. But we have evidence, and we suspect that your union and other unions, specifically the International Brotherhood of Drivers, the Airline Pilots Association, the Brotherhood of Railroad Workmen and the International Stevedores Association, are planning to harm this nation in such a way that neither the nation nor the union movement would survive.'

'I never wanted to hurt the country,' said Jimmy McQuade honestly.

And the two agents questioned him until dawn. They got his agreement to put two more men on the job. Themselves.

'That'll be dangerous,' said Jimmy McQuade.

'Yes. We think it may well be.'

'Okay. I never wanted to hurt anybody. I always thought unionism was protecting the working man.'

'That's what we think, too. This is something else.'

'We're going back tomorrow.'

'You're going back today.'

'My men are beat.'

'It's not us who are going to do the forcing. You can reach us at this number and we'll be ready when you get your crew together. Don't forget to leave out two of your regular men.'

The agents were right. Shortly after ten that morning, the vice-president of the International Communications Workers came to his door.

'What the hell are you doing, wildcatting, you sonuvabitch!'

'Wildcatting? My men were dying on their feet.'
'So they're soft. They'll get in shape.'
'They got out of shape on this job.'
'Well, you get them the hell back there if you know what's good for you.'
And Jimmy McQuade got his men the hell back there, knowing all along what the vice-president meant. Only this crew had two men who seemed to be doing a lot of strolling through the building together.
And their tool box contained a 35-millimeter camera with a telephoto lens. The day's work went well enough, considering that Jimmy McQuade was two men shy. At twelve hours Jimmy McQuade split the group into two shifts, asking one to be back in eight hours and the other to continue to work. The two men who did a lot of strolling and talking to other workers, were with the first group.
The last he saw of them, they were getting on the elevator.
Just before he was about to knock off for his eight hours in the early morning, the builder dropped by his floor.
'Come with me,' he said.
They took the closed elevator, the one the workers were not allowed to use. The builder pushed a combination of floors and Jimmy McQuade wondered who else would be getting on the elevator at the floors for which the buttons called. But the elevator did not stop. It continued down past the basement a good three floors. And Jimmy McQuade was afraid.
'Hey. Look. I'll get the job done. You don't have to worry about the job getting done.'
'Good, McQuade. I know you will.'
'Cause I'm a good worker. The best crew chief in the whole telephone system.'
'I know that, McQuade. That's why you were chosen.'
Jimmy McQuade smiled, relieved. The elevator door

opened to a large room two stories high with maps of America stretched end to end across the wall, a football-field-size America with the Rockies jutting perpendicularly from the wall like a hunchbacked alligator.

'Wow,' said Jimmy.

'Pretty nice,' said the builder.

'Yeah,' said Jimmy. 'But something puzzles me.'

'Ask away,' said the builder.

Jimmy pointed to the bottom of the map, and the auto-length sign with brass letters as high as desks.

'I never heard of the International Transportation Association.'

'It's a union.'

'I never heard of that union.'

'It's not going to exist until April 17. It's going to be the biggest union in the world.'

'I'd like to see that.'

'Well, that will be a little problem. You see, McQuade, in about ten minutes, you're going to be a puddle.'

The secretary of labor and the director of the Federal Bureau of Investigation finished their reports to the President. The three were alone in the Oval room.

The secretary of labor, a pudgy, balding man with professional bearing, spoke first.

'I think a union combining the major transportation unions, a supertransportation union, is impossible in the United States,' said the secretary of labor.

The director of the Federal Bureau of Investigation shuffled his papers and leaned a bit closer to the edge of his seat.

The secretary of labor talked on. 'The reason I think so is very simple. The drivers, the pilots, the stevedores, and the trainmen don't have that much central self-interest. In other words, they work for different employers. Moreover, the union leadership of each of these unions has vital concerns with its own sphere of influence. I cannot see four major union presidents willing to give up their own freedom of action. Just impossible. The wage scales of the workers are so different. A pilot makes just about three times what the others make. The membership will never go along. I know the drivers for instance. They're independent. They even dropped out of the AFL-CIO.'

'They were kicked out, weren't they?' said the director of the FBI.

The President raised a hand.

'Let the secretary finish.'

'Legally they were kicked out. Actually they dropped out. They were told to do certain things or face expulsion. They refused, and the rest was formality. They're an independent breed. Nobody is going to get the International Brotherhood of Drivers into another union. Nobody.'

The President looked down at his desk, then back at his secretary of labor. The room was cool, its temperature controlled by an elaborate thermostat that maintained the exact temperature the President wanted. The thermostat was reset every four years. Sometimes every eight years.

'What if the drivers are the union behind this?' asked the President.

'Impossible. I know the current president of that union personally, and no one is getting him, not even us, into an agreement whereby he loses freedom of action.'

'What if he's not reelected at this convention coming up?'

'Oh, he's going to win. He's got, excuse the pun, all the horses.'

'If he has all the horses, why was the convention suddenly shifted to Chicago? April 12 to April 17 is not exactly Chicago weather. Permit me a little pun, April in Chicago. I've never heard a song about it.'

'These things happen,' said the secretary of labor.

'Well, we all know for a fact, that the current president

of the drivers wanted Miami. He didn't get Miami. Las Vegas was mentioned, and then in a joint council meeting of their state and area leaders, the convention was moved to Chicago. Now, what if a supertransportation union just happens? Tell me the effects.'

'Oh, my Lord,' said the secretary of labor. 'Off the top of my head I would say it would be horrible. A disaster. Given some time to study it, I would probably say that it would be worse than a disaster. The country would just about close down. There would be a food crisis. There would be an energy crisis. There would be a run on the banking reserves to offset stagnated business like there has never been before. We would have a depression because of layoffs from inoperative factories combined with an inflation because of the scarcities of goods. I would say it would be like closing the arteries on a human being. Killing the flow of blood. If all the transportation unions struck jointly as one, this country would be a disaster area.'

'Do you think if you controlled such a union you could get all its members what they wanted?'

'Of course. It's like holding a gun to the head of everyone in the nation. But if this ever happened, there would be legislation from Congress.'

'The kind of legislation that would kill unionism and collective bargaining, correct, Mr. Secretary?'

'Yes, sir.'

'So either way this situation is highly undesirable.'

'It is as undesirable as it is improbable,' said the secretary of labor.

The President nodded to his director of the FBI.

'It's not all that improbable, Mr. Secretary. There have been strong financial links between the leaders of the pilots, stevedores, and trainmen with a dissident element of the drivers' union. These links began emerging roughly two months ago. It is this dissident element of the drivers which pushed for, and got, the convention to move to Chicago. Moreover, it is this dissident element that has constructed a large ten-story building just outside Chicago at incredible expense because of the rush aspects of contruction. Incredible expense. We don't know for sure where they got the money. We don't know for sure how they get things done so smoothly, but get things done they do. We have investigated the building and are continuing to attempt to do so. We cannot prove it yet, but we believe two of our agents who are missing were murdered in that building. We have not found their bodies. We have suspicions as to how the bodies are disposed of, but no confirming evidence, as yet.'

'Well, that settles it,' said the secretary of labor. 'No superunion about to be born can survive the murder of two FBI agents. You put all the leaders on trial. There's your superunion right there, doing life in Leavenworth.'

'We need evidence, which we hope to get. There is the jury system, Mr. Secretary.'

'There is that,' said the secretary of labor. 'There is that. As you gentlemen know, I am scheduled to address Friday's closing meeting of the convention. I don't know if I should go ahead with it. I did know there would be representatives there from other unions, but I never imagined it was anything like this.'

'Go ahead with your speech,' said the President. 'Go ahead as if nothing has happened, as if you know nothing of what we talked about. Mention this meeting to no one.' And to the director, 'I want you to withdraw all your men from this investigation.'

'What?' exclaimed the director, shocked.

'That's what I said. Withdraw your men and forget about this case and discuss it with no one.'

'But we've lost two agents.'

'I know. But you must do what I ask now. You must trust me, that it will work out well.'

'In my report to the attorney-general, how will I explain that we are not investigating our agents' disappearance?'

'There will be no report. I would like to tell you what I

am going to do, but I cannot. All I can say is that I have said too much. Trust me.'

'I have my men to worry about, too, Mr. President. Abandoning an investigation after we have lost two agents will not go down too well.'

'Trust me. For a while, trust me.'

'Yes, sir,' said the director of the FBI.

When the two men were gone, the President left the Oval room and went to his bedroom. He waited a few seconds to make sure no maid or butler was around, then unlocked the top bureau drawer. He reached his hand into the drawer and closed it around a small red phone. The phone had no dial, just a button. He glanced at his watch. This was one of the hours he could reach the contact.

The phone buzzed at the other end and a voice came on.

'Just a minute. That will be all, gentlemen. You're dismissed.'

The President heard other men, further from the receiver, objecting – something about in-patient treatment. But the man with the receiver was firm. He wished to be alone.

'You can be incredibly rude, Dr. Smith,' said one of the men in the distance.

'Yes,' said Dr. Smith.

The President heard mumbling, then a door shutting.

'All right,' said Dr. Smith.

'You are probably more aware of this than I am, but I fear that we face some trouble on the labor front that will cripple the entire nation to an incredible extent.'

'Yes. The International Transportation Association.'

'I've never heard of it.'

'You never will if, as we hope, everything works right.'

'This is a joining of unions into one superunion?'

'That's right.'

'So, you are on it?'

'Yes.'

'Are you going to use that special person? Him?'

'We have him on alert.'

'This is certainly drastic enough to use him.'

'Sir, there's no point in keeping this conversation going, even over a line as secure as this. Good-bye.'

TWO

His name was Remo, and he felt mildly sorry for the man who had erected the poorly hidden detection devices outside this elegant Tucson estate. It was such a good try, such a sincere effort to construct a deadly trap, yet it had one obvious flaw. And because the builder did not appreciate this flaw, he would die that day, hopefully before 12.05 P.M.—because Remo had to get back to Tucson early for important business.

The electric beams, functioning very similarly to radar, were rather well concealed and appeared to cover the required 360-degree ring which is supposed to be perfect for a single plane. The land was cleaned of just the kind of clump shrubbery that afforded concealment to attackers. The X layout of the ranchhouse, seemingly an architectural eccentricity, was actually a very good design for cross fire. The estate, though small and pretty, was a disguised fortress that could most certainly stop a mob executioner or could, if it came to it, delay a deputy sheriff—or two or ten.

If it ever came to it—because there was no chance that a sheriff or a state trooper would ever besiege this estate outside of Tucson. The man called Remo was now very simply penetrating the one flaw in the entire defense: The builder had not prepared for the eventuality of one man walking up to the front door by himself in broad daylight, ringing the doorbell, then executing the builder along with anyone else who got in the way. The estate was designed to prevent a concealed attack. Remo would not even be stopped as he walked past the beams in the open Arizona sun, whistling softly to himself. After all, what danger could one man be?

If Mr. James Thurgood had not been so successful in his business, he would probably live to see 1.00 P.M. Of course, if he were not so successful, he would be seeing 1.00 P.M. every day from the inside of a federal prison.

James Thurgood was president of the Tucson Rotary, the Tucson Civic League, a member of the President's Panel on Physical Fitness and executive vice-president of the Tucson Civil Rights Commission. Thurgood was also one of the leading investment bankers in the state. His profits were too big. After several layers of insulation, his money fueled the heroin traffic at a rate of $300 million a year. It returned a greater yield than land development or petrochemicals, and for James Thurgood—until this bright, hot day—had been just about as safe.

Between Thurgood and the neighborhood fix was the First Dallas Savings and Development Corporation, which lent large sums to the Denver Consolidated Affiliates, which made personal loans to people who needed them very quickly and in large amounts, one of them being recently Rocco Scallafazo.

Scallafazo offered no collateral, and as for his credit rating, it wasn't good enough to be bad. It was non-existent, since no one had ever given him a loan before. Denver Consolidated transcended the narrow regulations of banking and dared risk capital where other institutions would not. It gave Scallafazo $850,000 on his personal signature.

Denver Consolidated never got back the money. Scallafazo was picked up later with a suitcase full of Denver Consolidated's funds as he attempted to purchase raw heroin in Mexico. Undaunted, Denver Consolidated made another unsecured loan of an equal amount to Jeremy Wills, who was arrested without the money but with a trunkful of heroin. The Scallafazos and Willses were always being picked up, but no one could tie the evidence legally to the First Dallas Savings and Development Corporation, James Thurgood, President. There was no way to get Tucson's leading citizen into court.

So this day the man who financed heroin in the southwest would be gotten out of court. Remo casually strolled up the sunbaked driveway, examining his nails. His appearance certainly gave no hint of danger.

He was just under six feet tall, with soft friendly brown eyes and high cheekbones, a bit thin except for his thick wrists. His gait was smooth and his arms flowed freely. He glanced at the far kitchen window and the far living room window—he was directly in between. He was being watched. Good. He didn't want to have to wait at the door.

He checked his watch. It was 11.45 A.M. now. He figured it would take him a good fifteen minutes to walk back to town, a half an hour for lunch, maybe a short nap, and he could get back to important work by early afternoon. He still did not know all the duties of a union delegate or the essential aspects of the Landrum–Griffin Bill, and 'Upstairs' had said he should be ready very shortly for something big. Upstairs had even told him to ignore the hit on Thurgood if it would take too much time away from studies of the union movement.

'I might as well do the hit,' Remo had said. 'It'll be a good break.'

So there he was, standing at the doorway of the X-shaped ranch-style home, with two men peering at him from windows right and windows left. He reached into one of the bulging pockets of his trousers and withdrew two plastic envelopes the size of flattened baseballs. They were the heroin packages he had ordered from Upstairs. They were, his little escape tools. Worked correctly, he could stroll away from this house without anyone phoning the police. And, more important, he could do it in the daylight and not miss any sleep. One didn't have to make a little project like this unpleasant.

Remo rang the doorbell. He could feel the eyes on him.

The door opened and a large man in white houseboy coat stood in the doorway, like a surprise wall. A small pistol, probably a ·24 caliber Beretta, was rather expertly strapped beneath his armpit, showing only the barest outlines.

'Yes,' said the man.

'Good morning,' said Remo sweetly. 'I've come to kill Mr. Thurgood. Is he in?'

The butler blinked.

'What?'

'I've come to kill Mr. Thurgood. Will you let me in please.'

'You're crazy.'

'Look. I don't really have all day.'

'You're crazy.'

'Be that as it may, I can't do my work from out here, so let me in, please.'

'You want a glass of water or something, sir?'

Remo transferred both shiny packages to his left hand, and seeing the butler's eyes follow the movement, went for the large man's throat with a free right hand. The flat, knifelike hand was out and back like the flicker of a frog's tongue scoring on a fly. The butler stood, stunned, his eyes wide. He reached for his throat. His mouth opened. It filled with blood. The butler emitted gurgling sounds, then collapsed, struggling for air.

'The quality of help nowadays,' said Remo disdainfully and stepped over the butler into the house. It was a beautiful home with sunken living room and polished stone floors and large paintings hung in museumlike profusion. Lovely.

A maid saw the fallen body of the butler and dropped her tray, shrieking. The man who had been at the window on the right came clipetting down a stone hallway, gun in hand. It was a heavy gun, probably a ·357 Magnum. Foolish. He should have utilized the distance and gotten off a shot. Not that it would have saved him, but at least he would have died making proper use of his weapon.

The man possibly still did not know that the butler, his throat crushed, had strangled on his own blood. Remo disposed of the gun by snapping the man's wrist with a downchop. Continuing the motion, Remo's elbow cracked into the man's nose, jolting him back. Returning his arm from the blow, Remo jammed the heel of his hand into the broken nose, sending bone splinters into the brain. Zip, zip, it was over like that, and the man tumbled forward like a sack of wet asparagus. Plop.

'Mr Thurgood. Mr. Thurgood. We're being attacked,' came a voice. Remo peered down the left hallway. A cowboy hat disappeared into a door. Well, so much for surprise.

'How many?' came another voice. It was deep and resonant with just a faint hint of a wide Boston 'A' floating in the clear western tones. Remo had heard the voice on identity tapes he had gotten from Upstairs. It was Thurgood.

'One, sir. That's why we let him through.'

'Dammit. Why didn't the help stop him?'

'Dead, sir.' Thurgood and the man in the cowboy hat were obviously talking across the hallway.

'Come out, come out, wherever you are,' sang Remo.

'Who is he?' asked Thurgood.

'Your friendly neighborhood assassin,' Remo called out.

'The man is mad.'

Remo eased down the hallway and spotted a door that moved ever so slightly, like a tremble. The cowboy hadn't entered that door. Thurgood was behind it. Nice. The door was slightly ajar, just a sliver open. Remo, silent, moved against the wall, out of the line of vision afforded by the crack between door and jamb. When he neared the door, he reached a hand far from his body and knocked quickly. Twice.

Two slugs tore through the door and thudded into the wall across the hall, clipping a grapefruit-sized hole in the plaster. Nice pattern.

'Argh,' called out Remo, collapsing to the floor with a thud. He stuck out his tongue crazily and rolled his eyeballs back into his head so that only the whites would show. He heard the door near him open.

'I got him,' said Thurgood. Steps, perhaps twenty yards away and coming close. Something hard, metallic, against his temple. Pushing. Rifle barrel. Too much weight for a pistol. Smell of shoe leather. One has remnant of cow dung. Floor cold on back. One standing over the right shoulder. Other standing near hip. Hand on chest. One kneeling. Pressure.

'Still breathing, but faintly. Nice shot, sir.'

'Where did I get him?'

'I don't know. I don't see the bullet hole. What'll we tell the sheriff, Mr. Thurgood?'

'That I shot an intruder, of course. What did you expect me to say?'

'He's got something in his hand.' Remo felt his fingers unfolded and the two plastic packages of heroin being removed. 'It's horse. Yeah. Looks like the powder. It is.'

'Dammit.'

'Maybe we could say he brought it, Mr. Thurgood. That's the truth.'

'No. Flush it down the toilet.'

'It's thirty grand worth, at least.'

'Flush it. I'm an investment banker, you ninny.'

'Yessir.'

Remo felt the gun barrel tremble slightly. He could wait no longer. Up came his right thumb, deflecting the barrel as a shot chipped into the stone floor. Following through on the hand motion, his body rose in a single smooth flow. His left hand, whipping like an unsprung car aerial, caught the fine face of Tucson's leading businessman flat. Like a shot. Splat.

'Ugh,' said Thurgood in shock.

Spinning through the blow, Remo brought an elbow up and around to where the cowboy should have been. He was. The elbow caught the armpit, separating the shoulder and driving into the collarbone. The collarbone cracked. The cowboy, ten-gallon hat and cow-manure shoes, went forlornly into the wall and collapsed in pain.

Remo checked the hallway. Clean. He turned to Thurgood.

'Regards from the turned-on generation, sweetheart,' said Remo, as two fingers of his right hand drove the testicles of James Thurgood, leading Tucson citizen and heroin financier, into the lungs. On their way, they took a good portion of the intestinal tract, some of which now gushed in a bloody flood from the mouth of the man the courts could not touch. Thurgood lurched forward to spend the last twenty seconds of his life in awesome agony.

The cowboy would live.

'Ooooh,' he groaned.

Remo looked around the hall. Where were the bags of heroin? He lifted up the cowboy who emitted a shriek. There they were. Remo knocked the cowboy into them. He waited for the cowboy to regain some clarity of mind. Then he pushed the bags of heroin under the cowboy's nose.

'I think you'll want to get this cleaned up before you phone the sheriff,' said Remo. One bag had been torn open. Remo opened the second also. In full view of the cowboy, he sprinkled the white powder along the Thurgood hallway until now unsullied by its touch.

For final measure, Remo sprinkled the last of the heroin over the Thurgood living room, grinding it into the deep pile rug with his heels. He flipped the empty plastic bags to a sofa and strolled to the door.

'So long, shitkicker,' he called out to the cowboy and left the X-shaped fortress which had, after all, only one serious flaw in its defense.

It was a pleasant, dry, invigorating day, on which a man could whistle to his heart's content, and the stroll back to Tucson was enjoyable. By the time he reached the city limits, Remo had worked up a thirst. He dropped into a hamburger stand for a cola and 'two with everything, to go. Thanks.'

While waiting for the burgers, he briefly reviewed his morning's reading on collective bargaining. Something big was going to come off in Chicago. And somehow it had to do with the union movement. That was all Upstairs had said.

Remo added an extra dose of ketchup to his hamburgers and consumed them almost in four bites, washing them down with large draughts of the dark, sweet cola.

As he wiped his mouth a strange thing happened. Numbness crept up his arms into his neck, immobilizing his face. He heard a woman shriek, and as the hamburger stand whirled crazily above him, everything became very black.

THREE

'Welcome, International Brotherhood of Drivers.'

The banner floated over the quiet convention hall, catching vagrant indoor breezes. Two men stood by the speaker's podium, one watching the banner, the other nervously watching him.

In three hours, the rows upon rows of silent, darkened seats would be filled with cheering, clapping men, big men, strong men, men who could handle the monster tractor trailers and men who could handle those men. It would be a big convention. It always was, and this year Chicago had won over Miami or Las Vegas.

They were big spenders, these union delegates, and it was not the least of surprises that just two months before the convention, it had been switched from the big spending towns to a midwest city. Many of the delegates were angry about that. They knew who was behind it.

Neither their anger nor the nervousness of his number-two man bothered the president of Local 873, Nashville, Tennessee, that morning. He was absorbed in air currents.

'I wonder where those breezes come from,' said Eugene Jethro. 'I wonder if some internal force we know nothing about is blowing that banner.' He was a young man, in his mid-twenties, and his long golden locks flowed to the shoulders of his green velvet suit. He was too young to be president of a driver local, they said. Too mod to be president of a driver local, they said. Too fresh to be president of a driver local, they said. But here he was, and his name would be entered for the presidency of the International Brotherhood of Drivers.

'What do you care about banners, Gene? In three hours this convention opens and we're gonna get eaten alive,' said the vice-president of Local 873, Nashville. He was Sigmund Negronski, a burly, squat man with forearms like bowling pins. 'We gotta win the election, or we're gonna do time.'

Gene Jethro put a hand to his chin. His face screwed into deep thought.

'I wonder if just thinking about it can make that banner blow one way or another? The discipline of the mind over the essence of matter.'

'Gene. Will you get off it? We gotta work some more strategy.'

'It's been worked.'

'I'm scared. Will you listen to me. I'm scared. We spent money we didn't have. We made deals we can't keep. We've made commitments with some very rough people. If you don't win the presidency, we'll do time. If we're lucky.'

'Luck has nothing to do with it, Siggy,' said Jethro. He smiled the now famous Gene Jethro smile, a boyish open grin the media had quickly taken a liking to and other driver officers had resented. It was too Kennedyish. It was too political. They were tough men, these drivers, and worked hard for their money. They distrusted flamboyance as much as eloquence. And Gene Jethro had both. In just three months he had risen dramatically to become a national power in the brotherhood. He had this mysterious ability to get done whatever had to be done.

An indictment against a driver official in Burbank, California? Phone Jethro in Tennessee. He could get it quashed in hours.

A dispute over loansharking at a terminal? Somehow this young kid from Appalachia could settle it. Passport trouble of a friend? Get Gene Jethro.

'I don't know what the kid's got, but he's got it,' was

the common refrain among driver officials. 'Of course he's still too young for anything big.'

Jethro beckoned his vice-president to the podium.

'Here it is,' he said. 'Imagine the hall with 2,000 delegates. Screaming. Applauding. And I'm here, and I've got them in the palm of my hand. And with them, the next step.'

'There's another step, Gene?'

'There's always another step.'

'How about the one at hand? How about the presidency? If we don't get it, we're going to jail. We built that building with funds from the international. Now we don't have that kind of money.'

'You think I don't know that you dear, sweet, dumb Polack.'

'Hey, lay off that. You know, Gene, you used to be a nice kid. You used to be a comer. I could see you making it in twenty years, making it big. People liked you. But in the last three months, I don't know what's happened to you? You gave up a sweet girl for that broad who hardly wears clothes. You moved out of your apartment into a split level job with a swimming pool. You talk funny now, you think funny now, and I'm beginning not to know you.'

'You never knew me, dumbo,' said Jethro.

'Well, then, you're going to jail alone.'

'We, Siggy. We.'

'We nothing, Gene. You. All I did was step down as president of the local so you could take over.'

'Is that all, Siggy?'

'Well, my daughter got that kidney machine and don't think I'm not grateful.'

'Is that all, Siggy?'

'Well, we got the porch and the new car and I have bread for my girl friend's place.'

'Is that all, Siggy?'

'Well, uh, yeah. That's all. It's enough. Don't get me wrong. But it ain't enough to go to jail for.'

Jethro stuffed his hands into the pockets of his green bell-bottoms. He spun to the dead microphone and boomed to a nonexistent audience.

'Fellow drivers and delegates to the 85th Annual Convention of the International Brotherhood of Drivers, I give you my local vice-president. He is a loyal man. He is a man who will stand with you through thick and thin, for better or for worse, in sickness and in health. And I will tell you why he will stand with you.'

'Aw, come off it, will you Gene?'

'I will tell you why he will stand with you. He has the best of all reasons to stand with you.'

'C'mon, Gene.'

'Because he doesn't want to be a puddle.'

Blood drained from the face of Sigmund Negronski. His lips became dry. He looked nervously around the empty auditorium.

'You really like to hurt,' said Negronski.

'I love it.'

'You never used to be like this. What happened?'

'I got a swimming pool, a Jaguar, a mistress, a manservant, and enough power to make this union jump. And some day, in the not too distant future, I'm gonna make the country jump. Jump like you jump, you dumb, pathetic, fat Polack.'

Sigmund Negronski stood in sullen silence. He had brought this kid along from driver to shop steward to business agent. And then just three months ago the kid had started to change. Nothing you would notice right away, just more relaxed, then smooth, then vicious. What bothered Negronski was that when this kid smiled, Negronski still liked him, although he knew he should hate him for the indignities he inflicted on the older man. He should flatten this arrogant kid like a tomato under a U-Haul-It. But he still liked him. And that rasped to the very marrow of his bones.

Negronski looked at the dead microphone and then at Jethro.

'We just better win this thing tomorrow,' said Negronski.

The sounds of striding men echoed through the convention hall—heavy men with heavy footsteps, marching almost in unison. Negronski peered out into the darkness over the rows of empty seats, into the large, dark, disinfectant-smelling auditorium.

'Jethro, you sonuvabitch, I'm here, you little twirp, and today is the day you get yours.' The voice was deep and harsh and echoed the wide Boston 'A.' It was Anthony McCulloch, president of Local 73, Boston. And it looked as if he had brought his delegates with him. Big men, burly men, they advanced like the Green Bay Packers line going out to lunch.

McCulloch himself stood six-feet-five, and Negronski knew that he weighed 320 pounds because at last year's convention they had all weighed themselves on a freight scale after a round of drinking and a round of betting. McCulloch had claimed he could guess anyone's weight within five pounds. And he had.

McCulloch, despite his friendliness when he drank, was a power in Eastern union politics, and a man Jethro would need if he ever hoped to get close enough to sell the presidency of the international.

'Hello, Siggy,' said McCulloch. 'Who's your faggy friend?'

'Hi, Tony,' said Nebronski.

'Well, well. Anthony McCulloch. Thank you for coming,' said Jethro.

'I didn't come here to promise you my support. I came here to tell you that a group of us here found out about that building outside the city.'

Jethro smiled. 'Ah, Anthony, Anthony,' he sighed. 'Why must you do everything I figure you will do? Why aren't you some real competition for me?'

McCulloch looked up to the speaker's platform, then back at the men following him. Negronski recognized three presidents, two joint council presidents and five business agents with the rep as good muscle. They all thought this remark by Jethro was rather puzzling. If it had been a threat, they would have laughed in his face, Negronski knew. But his arrogance was only confusing. They obviously did not think of him as a threat.

'Kid,' said McCulloch. 'You may claim some kind of mental disorder before some judge, but we don't buy that plea. You stole union money, promised union money, our money, to put up some kind of a building outside this city. Without the okay of the council. Without even the written okay of the treasurer of the international, you committed us to millions. Millions, we still don't know how much. Our accountants are checking it out.'

'You spoke to the treasurer?' asked Jethro sweetly.

'Yeah. We spoke,' said McCulloch.

'And how is he?'

'He'll be walking again by maybe fall. Which is more than we can say for you. You're looking at some people you can't buy, kid. You're looking at people you can't deal for. We've had you, boy. We're gonna run your ass the hell out of the brotherhood.'

Little sounds of 'tell 'em,' 'you said it,' 'sock it to him,' could be heard from the group. The convention hall was chilly, waiting for the multitude of warming bodies, but Negronski felt perspiration form on his forehead. He wiped it off. His lips were dry again, and he did not know what to do with his hands.

'You part of this, Siggy?' asked McCulloch.

Negronski looked down at his shoes, back up to McCulloch, and then to Jethro, who lounged against the microphone like a rock singer. Negronski looked back down at his shoes.

'You part of this thing, Siggy?' McCulloch asked again.

Negronski mumbled an answer.

'I didn't hear you,' McCulloch said, 'You can still get off the hook, Siggy. We know you're okay.'

'I'm part of this thing,' said Negronski softly.

'What?' asked McCulloch.

'I'm part of it. I'm part of it,' yelled Negronski.

'I'm sorry to hear that, Siggy,' said McCulloch. 'Sorry for you.'

Jethro laughed and fondled the microphone head.

'You want to see where your money went?' he asked tauntingly.

'This pineapple is not to be believed,' said McCulloch to his men. 'And he wants to be president of the international.' The McCulloch people laughed.

They stopped laughing forty minutes later when their Cadillacs drove up Nuihc Street, and they saw the building, glistening aluminum spires reaching into a cloudless blue sky. Green sun-windows a story and a half each. Shiny bronze arches over the windows reflecting the sun like daylight torches. They gasped at its beauty.

Even Rocco 'the Pig' Pigarello, business agent for Local 1287, Union City, New Jersey, one of the roughest locals in the country where no local president ever left office on his feet, could not contain himself.

'It's byoootiful,' he said. 'Real byootiful.'

'You guys ought to like it. You paid for it. Triple what it would have cost if it had been put up in a reasonable time.'

'Byootiful,' said the Pig.

'We need it like we need leukemia. What do we need it for? It's our money and we don't need it.' McCulloch said.

'Yeah, we don't need it,' said the Pig. 'It's byootiful.'

'That's just the outside. Wait until you see the inside,' said Jethro. And the New England representatives became the first union delegates to view the inside of the building on Nuihc Street.

Rocco 'the Pig' Pigarello emitted 147 more 'byootifuls.' This was known because Timmy Ryan, Joe Wolcyz and Prat Connor kept count.

'You say "byootiful" once more, Pig, and you're going to be saying it without teeth,' said Connor.

'Yeah,' said the Pig. 'And you're gonna be hearing it without a head.'

'Hold it. Hold it. Don't fight,' said McCulloch. 'We got the pineapple to deal with first.'

Siggy Negronski, secreted a lead pipe under his jacket. It looked like the end of the line.

'You want to see me all at once in my office, or one at a time?' said Jethro.

'I'll see you first. There won't be any need for anyone else. Pig, Prat, Timmy, you guys, keep an eye on Siggy,' said McCulloch.

'We'll take the elevator to my office,' said Jethro.

'We'll settle it right here,' said McCulloch.

'My office is the biggest surprise,' said Jethro.

'Let's see the office,' said the Pig. 'What would it hurt to see the office?'

McCulloch shot Pigarello a dirty look. 'All right. We will go to the byootiful office.' His men laughed.

Nine driver officials in an elevator meant to hold a dozen normal-sized people was like packing a small hat box with a fifteen-pound ham. Negronski's hidden lead pipe was discovered immediately by feel. It was brought out from under his jacket rather roughtly, taking a piece of his jaw with it. The blood trickled down his neck and onto the shirt of his assailant. Negronski said nothing. It was all over.

'Siggy, baby. You just point out the dude who did that to you. We'll settle, baby. Nobody does that to one of my people,' called out Jethro.

But Negronski could not see his president in the crush. Jethro was the smallest man in the elevator, and he was hidden somewhere, Negronski believed behind McCulloch and the Pig. Although Jethro would have to be visible because he had seen what happened with the pipe. Negronski tried to turn his head to see where Jethro was. His face was slapped back into place. Maybe the two of them would just get a beating and then go to jail. Maybe that would happen. Negronski told himself that all the way to the basement floor.

The elevator doors opened on a large room and the men burst into it like the exploding of a sausage skin.

McCulloch cast a disdainful eye at the large map with the strange union title, and demanded to know where Jethro's office was.

'Over there,' said Jethro. McCulloch grabbed the smaller man by the back of his shirt collar and hustled him to the door at which Jethro had pointed.

'It's locked,' said Jethro.

'We'll go through it,' said McCulloch and pounded the smaller man into the door. It did not budge.

'It's got to be opened. Let me open it at least,' said Jethro. His body was twitching from the blow, but he managed to turn the handle first right, then left, then right all the way around and the door opened.

McCulloch threw the body into the room. 'I'll be out in five minutes, fellas,' he yelled. 'Watch Siggy. No rough stuff yet. He's got stuff to tell us,' yelled McCulloch.

With a hearty chuckle he went into the room and closed the door behind him. Negronski was quiet, avoiding the eyes of the other driver toughs. When he looked up finally, he noticed they were avoiding his eyes, too. If they waited long enough, Negronski hoped, maybe they wouldn't have the heart to finish him. Maybe not even work him over. They waited for what seemed a half hour. There was a good reason for this. It was a half hour.

Negronski felt his jaw. Pigarello handed him a handkerchief.

'Cold water would be good on that,' said the Pig, shamefaced.

'Yeah,' said Negronski. 'Cold water would be good.'

'You got any cold water down here? I mean not far.'

'No water in the basement.'

'You got water. Look at those pipes.'

'They're not for water.'

'What are they for?'

'I don't know. But they're not for water.'

'Yeah. But they look like water pipes. Don't they look like water pipes, fellas? I mean those are water pipes. Right?' said the Pig.

'Shut up,' said Connor. 'Just shut up.'

'They look like water pipes to me,' said the Pig, resigned to the peculiar emotional outbreaks of his cohorts.

The door opened. Out popped the shaggy head of Gene Jethro.

'Uh, McCulloch wants to see you, Connor. You're the one who swiped Siggy.'

'He had a pipe,' said Connor.

'Right,' said Jethro sweetly. 'I understand. C'mon in. McCulloch has something to tell you.'

Maybe, just maybe, Jethro's old charm had worked. Beautiful. Negronski didn't even feel any animosity towards Connor. These things happened. Negronski wasn't one to hold grudges. Everything would work out fine.

'Whaddya think happened?' asked Ryan.

'I don't know, maybe they made a deal,' said Wolcyz.

'Nah. McCulloch ain't making deals with that fag,' said another union delegate.

'He ain't not making any deals,' said another.

'He's making a deal,' said Wolcyz, suddenly smiling at Negronski.

'I know exactly,' said Pigarello. 'I know exactly.'

Everybody looked at the Pig.

'Those are definitely water pipes,' said the Pig. 'Those are water pipes. They're even sweating.'

'Drop dead,' said Wolcyz. 'Jeez,' said Ryan. 'Those aren't water pipes,' said Negronski. Another half hour passed. The door opened.

'Won't you gentlemen come in, please?'

The group nodded, and like schoolboys lining up for their turns at bat, all filed into the office.

'We got a deal,' whispered Wolcyz.

But there was no deal apparent. The room, about three times the size of the elevator, was bare but for an iron desk. One small bulb cast an inadequate yellow light in the room, making the pipe endings and nozzles on the wall seem like eerie extensions of shadows. McCulloch and Connor were nowhere around and there was no other exit. No window or door.

'McCulloch and Connor said they preferred Miami Beach. They didn't like modern ideas. They've left,' said Jethro.

'How'd they go out? There's no other exit,' said Wolcyz looking around the one-door, windowless room.

'They've gone. Now, lets get down to business. You gentlemen are the blocks to my presidency. Do you want to be rich or do you want to be left behind in the moribund, reactionary, penny-pinching practices of the previous regimes?'

'We ain't voting without McCulloch and Connor,' said a driver president from Maine.

'Then you'll never vote, baby,' said Jethro sweetly.

This proved not to be so because suddenly it became obvious to all what had happened. Immediately, the motion was unanimously passed, by voice vote, that the New England bloc did not wish to be left behind in the moribund, reactionary, penny-pinching practices of the old regime.

'The best throw is Jethro,' shouted one of the delegates, repeating a slogan he had seen on a batch of circulars he had thrown away the week before. He wished he had them now.

'Go with Jethro. The best throw is Jethro,' chanted the other delegates.

Gene Jethro quieted his new admirers. 'Gee, fellas. I don't know what to say. I guess a new consciousness has come to the International Brotherhood of Drivers.'

Pigarello had one question. It still bothered him.

'Mr. Jethro,' he said. 'Are they or aren't they water pipes coming into this office?'

'They're water pipes, Pig,' said Jethro.

Pigarello beamed. 'See. I told you.' He was so happy he even offered to take out the garbage since there didn't seem to be any janitors around the building as yet, and Mr. Jethro had two big plastic Garby bags sitting by the door.

FOUR

The doctor stared at the dying man who lay on a white padded table breathing faintly, the surgical lamps casting a pale glow on his trim body. If one were to look at him like this in the white tiled room with the surgical sinks and medical instruments, one would think he was looking at a normal human being about to undergo an operation.

One would also think he was in a hospital. But Dr. Gerald Braithwait knew better. He stared at the patient who in occasional moments of consciousness called himself Remo.

If this were a normal person, he would say the man was in shock. The pulse was irregular. The temperature was down. And the breathing was chaotic. Shock. But the patient recovered briefly every so often, as if he were not in shock, and the proper medical treatment for shock had only produced in this person a dangerous closing in on death.

Dr. Braithwait shook his head. He started to say something to the nurse, to tell her, to tell someone, anyone in this insane Alice in Wonderland madhouse, the problems this patient faced. The beginning of a word came out, then nothing. That would be useless also. The nurse did not speak a word of English.

But why should Dr. Braithwait be surprised? This wasn't even a hospital. Nothing was what is seemed. From the outside, this was a coal barge anchored in the mouth of a river in some southern state. He believed it was southern because he had seen the stars before the plane landed at a small airport which had not signs and no other airplanes. Just a helicopter to take him to a coal barge in the mouth of a river. When one walked through an opening in the pile of coal, one was immediately in a small hospital. One should have started complaining then, but when one is greedy for a cherished dream one does not start questioning until it is too late.

Dr. Braithwait looked at his nurse, an eastern European of some sort. He could not place the language.

The patient moaned. Dr. Braithwait signaled that the steel-belted straps on the ankles and wrists should be replaced. One did not want to witness another performance by this patient. Yesterday, he had fallen off the table. That was bad. He could have hurt himself. He did not. That was shocking. The patient was semi-conscious, and in midair, like a cat, turned his body to land on his hands and feet. Human beings did not do that. They did not turn like cats in midair.

But why should Dr. Braithwait be surprised? Only the body looked human. The nervous system, as Dr. Braithwait had discovered when he first stepped into this bad, bad dream, was not that of a human. The cells were human. The structure was human. But so enlarged were some aspects of the nervous system, so supersensitive, that it was not the human nervous system at all.

Dr. Braithwait pointed to the straps again. He smiled, not a sincere smile, but an indicator that he wished something done. The nurse smiled back. She applied the straps. The steel straps were on hand. Dr. Braithwait didn't have to order those. They were shown him by that Dr. Smith first day on the barge during a tour of the hidden hospital with room for twenty and a staff of three: Dr. Smith, the nurse who did not speak English, and that incredible, insane old Oriental.

'The normal restraining straps are already on this table,' Dr. Smith had said. 'But we have others that are stronger.'

'No need,' Dr. Braithwait had said. 'Nobody can break out of one of those straps. Veterinarians have even used them for gorillas.' Oh, how foolish he had been. The normal straps had broken the first day.

Dr. Braithwait stared at the shiny steel webbing being snapped to the large wrists. Dr. Smith was behind all this. Dr. Smith's reputation would be mud when word of this ... this kidnapping got out.

It was a kidnapping, dammit, even if Dr. Braithwait had agreed. It was a kidnapping across state lines if ever there was one. Dr. Braithwait clenched his fists. He noticed that the nurse looked worried. He forced a smile to indicate he was not mad at her.

Dr. Harold Smith, director of Folcroft Sanitarium in Rye, New York, had a fine reputation. And this reputation would not be so fine when Dr. Braithwait got out of this hospital that was disguised as a barge. He would tell the whole world what had happened to one of the nation's foremost internists.

It had all seemed so harmless, and yes, well, profitable, too. If Dr. Smith hadn't known about Dr. Braithwait's special plan, or hope, or even a dream one could call it, Dr. Braithwait would never have agreed to examine a special patient right away, a patient who was 'Just a short hop from Folcroft.' But Dr. Smith had known of the dream. He had known and had promised to make it come true. An entire medical school built around the concepts Dr. Braithwait knew were valid, needed, and sure to be successful—concepts that had yet to be tried by others. Concepts that Dr. Braithwait, in his thirty years as one of the country's leading internists, had formulated. Dr. Braithwait should have been suspicious when Dr. Smith phoned his office in New York City and immediately, or almost immediately, offered him the hospital. Oh, wouldn't it be nice if Dr. Braithwait could drop up to Folcroft this afternoon for a little chat about the medical school? Oh, wouldn't it be nice if preliminaries could be worked out right away, because Folcroft was interested in this new concept also?

How did Dr. Smith hear about the new concepts for a medical school when Dr. Braithwait had told only a few friends? That's a long story. That's something Dr. Braithwait should talk about when he got to Folcroft. And Dr. Braithwait wouldn't even have to drive. There was a driver in New York City who worked for the sanitarium and would be happy to take Dr. Braithwait right now.

Did Dr. Braithwait stop to think? Did Dr. Braithwait become suspicious? Did Dr. Braithwait respond like a mature, intelligent human being? No. Dr. Braithwait thought only about the medical school, wrapped his plans in a giant paper bundle, and canceled his appointments for the afternoon.

That was the first step. The second, for some unexplained reason, was a medical examination. Dr. Braithwait agreed to it. Another internist of equal rank was having an examination also.

'Hey, Gerry. Gerald Braithwait. How are you doing?'

'Fine. Fine,' Dr. Braithwait had said.

'This Folcroft is some place. They've got money coming out of their ears.'

'Is that so?' said Dr. Braithwait. 'Is that so?'

Dr. Smith seemed incredibly interested in the new hospital. He even talked dates of construction. But he was in a rush. Could the sanitarium's private plane take Dr. Braithwait back to New York City? They could discuss the new medical school on the airplane.

Of course, agreed Dr. Braithwait. That was the third step. The plane did not land in New York City. Almost as soon as it took off from the small Westchester airport, two things happened. One, Dr. Smith promised the medical school. Two, would Dr. Braithwait examine a patient Dr. Smith was very concerned about. He was just south of New York, and if Dr. Braithwait could look at him now, Dr. Smith would be ever so grateful.

Fourth and final mistake.

'Yes, Dr. Smith. I would be delighted.'

Just south was a two and a half hour trip with night falling rapidly. At the airport, it was just a few minutes by helicopter. The copter landed on top of a broad pile of coal. Dr. Braithwait could smell the swampiness of the nearby lands. Breezes brought salt water air. It was a river near the ocean.

And then into the hole in one of the coal piles and the door locked behind him, and Dr. Smith was not all that friendly anymore.

'You will cure this patient,' said Dr. Smith. 'I can be reached through a telephone you will find in a room down the hall.'

A cursory tour of this hospital and then Dr. Smith was gone, and here was Dr. Gerald Braithwait for nearly a week, trapped in a madhouse with a nurse who did not speak English, a patient who only resembled a human being, and an Oriental who spoke English but made no sense.

Dr. Gerald Braithwait watched the body twitch.

'I think the straps will hold,' he said.

The dark-eyed nurse looked at him, puzzled. He pointed to the straps, made a tugging motion and smiled. The nurse smiled back. Wonderful. Sign language.

If only that peculiar old Oriental, obviously three breaths from the grave, also failed to speak English. That would be a help. He was a nuisance from the first day, when he hovered over the body, watching, probing with his long fingernails, staring at the doctor with distrust. He had explained to Braithwait what happened.

'Hamburger,' the old man had said. 'An impurity in his essence.'

'Will you get out of here?' Dr. Braithwait had said. 'How can I examine a patient with you poking him?'

'My son took an impurity into his essence,' insisted the ancient Oriental. 'It must be removed.'

Dr. Braithwait had called for an orderly to remove the old man. There was none. He tried to do it himself. He pushed. The frail creature did not move. He grabbed a shoulder. The shoulder seemed to slip from his hands. Dr. Braithwait pushed on the chest. The old man couldn't have weighed a hundred pounds, but he did not move. Dr. Braithwait weighed a middle-aged 195 pounds, or about that. He had been losing weight for the last month. Dr. Braithwait had shoved again, and again no movement.

Then, feeling the rising anger coupled with the ever present frustration of the situation, he had hurled himself into the frail wisp of a man. And bounced off. Backside on floor. Bounced off.

'You are most fortunate that I need your services,' said the old man. For the next few days he stayed beside the table upon which the patient rested, watching the doctor, watching the patient, asking questions about this instrument or that.

'All right,' he said finally. 'Perhaps you will be able to save him.' And with that he was out of the room and down the corridor and had not been seen since.

The patient was a horror of reflexes. A touch on one muscle produced a whole series of responses, as if the muscles had been given a memory or had been programmed. A tap on the knee generated a flurry of hand movements so fast they appeared to be a blur.

And the semiconscious babbling. If one were to believe the delusions, this man had been publicly electrocuted so that he could be transformed into a sort of super-weapon without a past, without an identity. There were fragments of statements such as 'Chiun,' 'That's the biz, sweetheart,' 'Jam the heart.'

The patient was obviously suffering from guilt through the delusion that he had killed scores of people. The patient babbled about balance and thrusts and peaks. The muscles twitched, the eyes opened, some consciousness, and then back to sleep.

Dr. Braithwait stared at the evenly breathing patient. What on earth was wrong with him? This defied medical knowledge.

The only clue available came from the old Oriental on the first day. Hamburger. Hmmm. Hamburger.

Dr. Braithwait absentmindedly touched the steel straps. Hamburger. He checked his watch. He had been warned not to disturb the Oriental until after 4.30 P.M. It was that now, Hamburger. That nervous system.

Dr. Braithwait strode quickly out of the room with the surgical lights and went down the corridor. He knocked on a door. He waited. Inside the mellifluous organ of a daytime soap opera whined its heavy tune. Then someone was selling soap. The door opened.

Draped in a saffron kimono, the aged Oriental indignantly inquired about Dr. Braithwait's manners, upbringing, and by what right he, Dr. Braithwait, felt he could destroy moods of artistry?

'That hamburger you claim did the damage. Where did the patient get it.'

'From filth, ignorance and stupidity.'

'No. The name of the place which sold him the hamburger.'

'The name is dog and son of dog. The name is Halloran's Happy Hamburgers.'

'That's it. Of course. Now I understand,' said Dr. Braithwait. 'With his nervous system, naturally he would become semicomatose.'

'Because of the impurity of the essence.'

'No. No. No. Monosodium glutamate. These hamburgers are nationally made for the entire Halloran chain. They're made of gristle and the worst sections of beef. They sell cheaply and to make them edible they're loaded with monosodium glutamate. Even some normal people have nervous system difficulties from it. That nervous system ... well. it just went into a semisleep.'

'You talk in riddles,' said the old man.

'You were right. It was something in the hamburger.'

'The impurity of the animal fat. The excessive indulgence. The lack of personal discipline.'

'No. Monosodium glutamate.'

The old man's face wrinkled into puzzlement.

'I tell you, the spiritual sone of the Master of Sinanju has violated the purity of his essence, clearly and simply and understandably, and then you tell me "monosodium glutamate." Now what are you talking about?'

'Monosodium glutamate is a chemical.'

The old man nodded.

'It is in food.'

The old man nodded.

'It was in the hamburger eaten by the patient.'

The old man nodded.

'Monosodium glutamate affects some nervous systems.'

The old man understood that.

'With the incredibly finely tuned nervous system of the patient, it wreaked havoc.'

The old man smiled. 'For a doctor, you are very stupid. I do not understand a word you say. Come. Let us go to my son. Is he better yet?'

'Not much, maybe today. Maybe tomorrow or the next day, but he will definitely recover.'

'I ask you a favor,' said the old man.

Braithwait listened respectfully.

'When I first explained to you what caused the harm, I accidentally said this white man was the true son of the Master of Sinanju, even though he was white.'

Braithwait nodded. He remembered that idiotic rambling.

'Do not let the patient know this. If he thinks he has any Korean in his soul, he will be impossible to live with. I call him white.'

'He is Caucasian,' said the doctor. 'I'd say Mediterranean—Northern Europe, a combination. High cheekbones may make him Slavic in there somewhere, but he is white.'

'I say that. Not you. You cannot call him white. Now do you understand? Simple, no?'

That evening when the patient was shrugging off the last effects of the monosodium glutamate, the old Oriental hummed happily. He kissed the forehead of the patient. He chuckled. He sang. He danced around the table. When the patient blinked his eyes and said. 'Where am I?' the old man suddenly flew into a rage, his frail, bony arms flailing.

'Dead. You should be dead. Ungrateful, horrible, undisciplined white man. You are a white man. You will always be a white man. You were born white and you will die a white man. White man with white man's hamburgers.'

'Jeez, Chiun, will you get off my back. What happened?' asked the patient. He looked at the straps and seemed amused. He looked at Dr. Braithwait.

'Who's the dingdong with the stethoscope?' he asked.

This infuriated the aged Oriental.

'Who this? Who that? What is this? What is that?' yelled the old man. 'Questions you have now. You have many questions about this and that, but you do not question what you put into your blood stream.'

Dr. Braithwait had had enough. He would be leaving soon, having told Dr. Smith that the patient was on the road to recovery. He would not have his office turned into a circus, even if it was hidden under piles of coal on a barge in a river.

'You there,' he said sternly to the patient, 'put your head back on the table.'

'Where am I, Chiun?' the patient asked, ignoring Dr. Braithwait.

'That is of great importance. That you ask. That you must know. You will die if you do not know that, Remo,' shrieked the Oriental called Chiun. There was triumph in his voice.

'Your name is Remo, correct?' said Dr. Braithwait. 'What's your last name?'

'What's yours?' asked Remo.

'I'm asking the questions. If you don't answer them, you'll stay strapped to the table.'

With a little laugh, and a flip of the body as graceful as

any ballerina's, the patient burst the bonds and was on the floor.

'Who is this guy, Chiun?'

'Who is your stomach? Aha. That is the question.'

The entranceway to the hidden hospital could be heard opening down the corridor. Purposeful strides. The door opening. Dr. Harold Smith, lemon face a mask of calm, entered.

'I could hear you outside the barge,' said Dr. Smith. 'Stop this racket.'

He looked balefully at the patient.

'Hmmm. Very good, Dr. Braithwait. I'd like to talk to you privately a moment, if you please.'

'I have a few words to say to you, too, Dr. Smith.'

'Yes. I'm sure you do. I will explain everything shortly. I'll meet you at the end of the corridor. I'd like to speak to the patient first a moment, if you please.'

Dr. Braithwait glowered at Smith.

'I will be at the room at the end of the corridor, and I will give you exactly ten minutes to complete explaining to me what this is all about,' said Dr. Braithwait. 'Ten minutes, Dr. Smith.'

Braithwait had nothing to pack or he would have packed. From the room he had slept in, he removed a small plastic bag containing an instrument made of metal and black plastic. It looked like an electric drill, but it did not use current. He jammed a vial of strong nerve depressant into the instrument. It was an automatic needle used for inoculating many people when a normal syringe would prove too time-consuming. The dose Dr. Braithwait set was close to fatal. He was not concerned with curing the recipient this time. He cared about living. And if he had to kill to live, he had that right. He eased the automatic needle under his white coat. It would shoot enough depressant to immobilize the recipient. For the strange patient whose nervous system had already undergone a severe testing, it would prove fatal. So be it.

Dr. Braithwait went to the small room at the end of the corridor and waited. Funny, they had supplied him this device on demand. He had merely called Smith, and within eight hours there was someone entering the barge with a package. Ah, such service. Perhaps there would even be the medical school he was promised. In which case the automatic needle would not have to be used. It was just a safety factor. In case.

From his seat, Dr. Braithwait could see Smith pace down the corridor, heavy footed, with a faint trace of a stoop to his shoulders as though he bore a heavy weight, unseen by anyone but the bearer. Dr. Smith entered the room and sat down. He avoided Dr. Braithwait's eyes. Finally, Dr. Smith looked directly at him.

'First, let me say, Dr. Braithwait. You were one of two choices. You met the other at Folcroft, another top internist. You have cancer of the stomach. He is in good health. You have maybe five years to live, depending on an operation. His probabilities of living are higher. So we chose you. That was the reason for the checkup at Folcroft. We're going to kill you, and I had intended to kill whomever we chose. I am going to tell you why you must die. It is unfair, I know. But we are in desperate straits. We have been since our inception. If America was not hanging on the ropes, we wouldn't have existed in the first place.'

Dr. Braithwait eased his hand under his white medical jacket and clutched the handle of the needle. It was moist and clammy.

'That's quite a lot to digest, Dr. Smith. I mean hearing about your own death like that.'

'I know. We could have killed you without your knowing it, with your walking out of the barge, with my apologies, with you holding plans to a new medical school, and then nothing. You would feel nothing. But I think your life has meant something, and I think your death should also.'

Dr. Smith sighed, and began.

'Quite a few years ago, it was decided by an American President—no longer living, by the way—that the country was headed for chaos, that crime was rising and would rise more rapidly. It was decided by this President that the United States Constitution did not work, that you could not have all those personal safeguards and maintain a semblance of civilization when so many, many people refused to obey the law. The American people is not that people. Right from the biggest corporations to the smallest hubcap thief, this nation is under assault and has been for a long time. That assault would have led, inexorably, to a police state.'

'It could have led to more freedoms,' said Dr. Braithwait bitterly.

'No. It is a fact of political science that chaos is invariably followed by dictatorship. The biggest freedoms exist during peaceful times. America as all of us knew it was dying. To combat this, the President could not himself violate the law, because that would prove the Constitution did not work. No. No existing enforcement agency could stem the tide under the Constitution. So the President did something else. He decided to give an edge to the survival of the nation. He decided that if the nation could not survive within the Constitution, he would create something outside the Constitution that made it work.'

'That's the same as violating the Constitution,' said Braithwait.

'Correct,' said Dr. Smith. 'But what if this organization did not exist?'

'I don't understand.'

'What if the organization did not exist in the government budget? What if only three people knew of it, what it did? What if the many people who worked for it did not know for whom they worked or why? What if its budget was siphoned off from half a dozen federal agencies? What if it just did not exist at all?'

'That's impossible. You can't have large numbers of

people working for an organization and not knowing it,' said Braithwait.

'That's just where you're wrong. I thought so, too, at the beginning, until I realized that the majority of the people working in America today only know whom they're working for because they're told.'

'That's absurd.'

'Whom are you working for?'

'Well, I have the hospital board, the director of the hospital, and I have a private practice.'

'The latter is self-employment. At the hospital, are you sure you are working for the board, or do you know because you have been told and see those people around?'

Dr. Braithwait ruminated on that statement. Dr. Smith continued.

'Now. Our main job is seeing that prosecutors get information they ordinarily wouldn't get. That crooked cops are exposed because someone just happens to talk, and there just happens to be public pressure. We even financed a novel about organized crime to expose it, to expose it to light. When a Mafia don set up a public organization to try to suppress the FBI, we generated friction within the ranks of organized crime. He was shot by his own kind. Only rarely do we ourselves kill. Then, because our secrecy is so necessary, only one man does the killing—one human being upon whom we rely. This lessens the chance of exposure. You see, for us to be exposed means a public admission by the government that the Constitution does not work. We cannot afford that. It would really mean that all our work is wasted.'

'What happens when that man gets arrested and his fingerprints are checked out?'

'Well, chances of anyone being able to contain him are slight, but he has no registered fingerprints.'

'You lifted that from the FBI?'

'No. We didn't have to. You see, the man you helped save does not exist. He has been publicly electrocuted. His files were transferred automatically. Our Destroyer, as we call him, is the most vulnerable of all of us, since he operates outside the confines of Folcroft, exposing himself to danger. No, he is one of the three who knows, and we could not possibly afford for him to have an identity. What better tool than a dead man.'

'His nervous system is unique.'

'Probably just about like Chiun's now. Chiun is his trainer.'

'I see,' said Braithwait. 'The Oriental knows, too.'

'No. He does not know exactly who we are, and he does not care. He gets paid. And the money is delivered where he wants it. He does not care who we are. He is probably the truest professional alive today.'

'And the third man?'

'Each incumbent President.'

'What happens when the President retires.'

'He tells the incoming President, and then himself never speaks of it again. We ask them to forget, and—you'd be surprised—they do.'

'What would prevent you from taking over the country?'

'We have built-in stops. And besides, our only attacking force is one man, and while he is unusual, he is no match for an army. His best weapon is, as he tells me, secrecy. In open warfare he'd be doomed. Just look at the conflict with Japan during the second world war. Certainly, man for man, the Japanese had more knowledge of the martial arts.'

Dr. Braithwait gripped the handle of the injection device. He felt a cold cunning he had never known before, a staring at his grave and not worrying. Just acting.

'You planned my murder right from the beginning when you phoned me, Dr. Smith, didn't you?'

'Yes.'

'Is that the way you protect a piece of paper? By violating it?'

'If a tree falls in the forest and no one hears it, does it make a sound?' said Dr. Smith.

In one smooth motion Dr. Braithwait pulled the needle device from under his jacket. Dr. Smith did not move. Dr. Braithwait saw the patient coming down the corridor and he brought the automatic needle to Dr. Smith's wrist. 'Don't move or you're dead,' he said.

Dr. Smith glanced briefly at the needle and then back at the patient as if the needle was of no import, as if Dr. Braithwait had placed a piece of peppermint against Dr. Smith's hand. But, as ordered, the latter did not move his hand.

'You're arithmetic is off, too,' said Dr. Braithwait. 'You said three men. What about the man who recruited your weapon?'

'He was injured,' said Dr. Smith, 'and exposed to a situation where he might talk. We had to kill him. All right, Remo. There's an automatic needle probably containing some poison pressed against my right hand.'

'Good,' said the patient smiling. 'Now you know what it feels like.'

'I'm going to kill him if you move any closer,' said Dr. Braithwait. His finger closed against the trigger of the needle.

The patient smiled and shrugged.

'That's the business, sweetheart,' he said. And then Dr. Braithwait could have sworn he saw a hand flash out to the needle. He was not sure, however, and he did not have time to press the trigger, because there was the beginning of the hand flash and then darkness.

Remo stood over the body watching its finger squeeze the trigger in obedience to the last command of the victim's brain. The fluid shot out in short needlelike bursts, making a spray, then a whitish puddle on the floor.

'Who was he?' said Remo.

'The man who saved your life,' said Dr. Harold Smith.

'You're a real sonuvabitch, you know that, Smitty,' said Remo.

'Do you think anyone else could run this organization?'

'No one else would want to,' said Remo. 'Guy saved my life, huh? Hmmm.'

'Yes, he did.'

'We pay off nice, don't we?'

'We do what we have to. Now get out of that silly nightgown. You're due in Chicago in a few hours. No labor leader ever wore a costume like that.'

FIVE

Remo followed the directions. He would meet Abe Bludner, president of Local 529, New York City, at the Pump Room in Chicago for breakfast. Bludner would be a squat, bald man with a face like a pocked watermelon.

Bludner, according to reports from Upstairs, had a stormy union record. He began driving at 15 with a forged license, became a shop steward at 23 when he singlehandedly fought off five company goons with a bailing hook, at 32 became the numbers bank for all barns (truck warehouses) in his local, and became president at 45 in an intralocal political battle that saw his predecessor lose by three votes in a case that wended its way through the courts for four years until the next election. Bludner won the second election handily and had been president of the local ever since. From time to time some of his drivers broke their arms when they accidentally fell into crowbars. Usually these crowbars were attached to Abe Bludner. From time to time trucking outfits would damage themselves when colliding with a crowbar. That is, the president or the treasurer or the vice president in charge of the terminal operations would find himself with very uncomfortable fractures. More often than not, the employer was the one who initiated the violence by hiring gangsters. Gangsters always met crowbars. After a while gangsters stopped coming.

From time to time many employers saved themselves the expense of renting hoodlums and dealt directly with their labor antagonist. They did this with envelopes. Fat envelopes. The proceeds of this corporate largesse often found its way to drivers whose hospital insurance had run out, drivers' children for whom the local's scholarship fund could not provide enough, and drivers who could not quite make a down payment on a mortgage. No member of the local was ever laid off for more than a day, and only one driver who belonged to the union was ever fired for cause. He had, for the third time, rammed a tractor trailer into the side of the barn while drunk.

Bludner pleaded with the owner to give the driver a nondriving job. The owner refused. Abe Bludner pointed out that the driver had four children and a wife. The owner refused. Abe Bludner said the driver had enough problems already. Wouldn't the owner reconsider? The owner would not. The next day, the owner saw the folly and hardheartedness of his ways. He wired the president of Local 529 that he had changed his mind. He would have come personally, dictated the owner, but he would not be out of hospital for a month and even then doctors were not sure if he would ever walk again.

Abe 'Crowbar' Bludner ran his local with a tight hand, an open pocket, and a heart as big as all outdoors—if you did your work and kept you face relatively clean. He was said to have never made a serious mistake.

Abe Bludner knew better. He had not seen fit to include the US Government in his list of beneficiaries from the gift envelopes. The US Government appeared not to know this until the day before the 85th annual convention of the International Brotherhood of Drivers.

Then Abe Bludner discovered that the Internal Revenue Service was deeply grieved at being excluded from his largesse. But Abe Bludner could set things right again, said the man 'from IRS.' Abe Bludner could show the bigness of his heart, by giving a young, deserving man a job with his local, by making this newcomer a business agent for Local 529 International Brotherhood of Drivers, New York City.

Abe 'Crowbar' Bludner outlined why this was impossible. A man had to be elected business agent according to union bylaws. His other men would resent someone coming in off the street and taking a major job. Abe Bludner had power because he didn't do such foolish things—things that would antagonize the very people he depended on for his power. So the IRS would have to ask for something else.

The something else, as it turned out, would be ten to fifteen years at the Lewisburg Federal Prison. Abe Bludner asked the name of his new business agent.

'Remo,' said the supposed representative from IRS.

'Johnny Remo, Billy Remo? What Remo?'

'Remo is his first name.'

'All right. That is a nice first name. May I have a last name to put in the union records.'

'Jones.'

'A lovely last name. I used it once in a motel.'

'So did I,' said the man supposed to be from the IRS.

Thus it was that on this sunny morning Abe Bludner waited for his new business agent and delegate to the convention.

He did his waiting with two other officials of his local who in other businesses would be called bodyguards. Remo saw them in a booth, sitting at a table laden with food, little cakes, glasses of beading orange juice, and cups of steaming black coffee.

Remo could smell the bacon and the home-fries from twenty feet away. So could his trainer, Chiun, who had been assigned by Upstairs to personally supervise his pupil's diet.

'I knew I shouldn't eat a hamburger, what I didn't know was that I *couldn't,*' Remo had said.

'Could and should are the same things for the wise man,' Chiun had said. 'I have taught you the pathetically basic rudiments of offense and defense. Now I must teach you to eat.'

And that was Chiun's assignment. As they approached the Bludner table, Chiun's face contorted in contempt for the awful smells of the food. Remo's mouth filled with delicious overwhelming desire. Perhaps he could sneak a roll.

'Mr. Bludner?' said Remo.

'Yeah,' said Bludner, a crisp, brown morsel of home-fry caught in the corner of his lips.

'I'm Remo Jones.'

Bludner tore an end off an onion roll and dipped the soft white interior into the golden, flowing egg yolks. He lifted the roll, dripping yellow over the brown crust dotted with white onion chips toasted black at their corners. Then he mouthed it, swallowing the roll morsel whole.

'Yeah, well, good to see ya,' said Bludner without enthusiasm. 'Who's he?'

'He's my nutritionist,' said Remo.

'What's the clothes he's wearing?'

'It's a kimono.'

'Well, sit down. Have you eaten yet?'

'No,' said Remo.

'Yes,' said Chiun.

'Well, have you or haven't you?' said Bludner.

'Yes and no,' said Remo.

'I don't know what that means,' said Bludner.

'It means I've eaten but it doesn't feel like it.'

'Well, sit down and have a coffee and Danish. I got your union credentials with me. This is Paul Barbetta and Tony Stanziani, stewards and delegates to the convention.'

There was a round of handshakes in which Stanziani attempted to crush Remo's hand. Remo watched the dark-eyed hulk squeeze almost to redness in face. Then with simple compression Remo strained Stanziani's thumb. He did this not because Stanziani had squeezed hard. Actually it would have been good for Remo to be thought of as weak. No, Remo hurt the thumb because of the Danish he could not have. Golden Danish in rings with brown chips of almonds and cinnamon filling. Rich cheese Danish, with creamy white, pungent filling. Cherry Danish with sweet red sauce.

Stanziani, despite his sudden pain, was really lucky he had a hand to take back.

'Ow,' said Stanziani.

'I'm sorry,' said Remo.

'You got a tack in your hand or something?' Stanziani blew on his thumb.

Remo opened his palms to show that nothing was in them.

'You guys want Danish and coffee?' said Bludner. 'I got a special Danish I make right here at the table. I'll be making it myself. It's called a "Dawn Danish." It's very nice. Named after my wife.'

'No. We don't want it,' said Chiun.

'What? Do you eat for him?' said Bludner. 'Look, it's going to be rough enough passing you off as a driver, I mean what with you looking kind of faggy, no offense. But you know you don't look as though you carry much weight and those clothes you're wearing are kind of, well, delicate, know what I mean? And if your nutritionist goes with you everywhere, I think we're going to be in some traffic, Remo. Know what I mean?'

'No,' said Remo.

'You don't look like a business agent. You look like a stockbroker or something. Like a clerk or a young vice president of a fashion company. Know what I mean?'

'I think so,' said Remo.

'I got a reputation and a certain prestige, and I don't want it to suffer. We're known as stand-up guys and it's good being known as that. Know what I mean?'

'No.'

'Okay. Let me give you a very brief and important history of our labor union. When we drivers first organized, companies would hire gangsters to drive us out. Tough guys. Pipes, guns, everything. So the drivers knew they had to be just as tough to survive. So only tough guys got to represent them, and you, well, you don't look tough. You look just, well, average, kind of. No offense. I think you'd make a great whatever you want to be, but you don't look the part of one of my boys, and I think there are going to be a lot of people feeling you out. Just stay close to Tony and Paul. They're stand-up guys and they won't let anything happen to you. Namely, they won't let you embarrass me.'

'Right, Abe,' said Tony and Paul in unison. 'You stay close to us, kid, and you'll be all right.'

'Not if he puts that filth in his stomach,' said Chiun.

'Well, he won't eat. Okay, Doc?' said Bludner. 'You stay with my boys, do whatever you have to do, then get out and we'll have your name off our books real fast. Right? You know the deal, right?'

Remo nodded. He knew the deal very well. Kill whoever's death would stop the giant transportation unions from joining. That was the base plan. The extreme plan was to eliminate the presidents of the four transportation unions, because without them the superunion would take years in forming again. And, of course, leave the blame on Abe 'Crowbar' Bludner, because only if the killings were an intraunion squabble, could the union movement go on. Should they be considered a management plot, the nation would never recover.

This was the driver's convention, but on Friday the three other union presidents would be on the speaker's platform to announce their joining, according to Smith's sources. So Dr. Smith's orders were simple. If it comes to that, kill them. All four. If it comes to that, you can even be seen. After all, when they know it is one of Bludner's boys, and he proves to be an import, who would ever believe that Abe 'Crowbar' Bludner had not imported a professional killer to do the job?

'I know the deal,' Remo said to Bludner.

Chiun watched a bacon strip go into Stanziani's mouth as if the man were swallowing a live snake. He watched the potatoes the same way. Then Bludner snapped his fingers.

'Now, you'll see it,' said Bludner. A waiter glided to

the table and leaned forward over the fresh daisies in a water-filled pitcher set on the white tablecloth.

'I wanna bowl of whipped cream,' said Bludner. 'I want some fresh cherries, pitted. I want some cherry preserves. I want a bowl of crushed nuts, almonds, cashews, maybe a couple peanuts crushed real good, and I wanna bowl of hot fudge. And bring some more round cinnamon Danish.'

The waiter repeated the instructions, being reminded that the nuts must be crushed fine, almost pastelike.

'You want one, Tony, and you want one, Paul, and you don't want one, Doc. How about you, Remo?'

'He doesn't want one,' said Chiun.

Bludner shrugged. Remo looked at the daisies.

'Who are you supporting for the election?' Remo asked.

'Jethro. Gene Jethro,' said Bludner dropping his fork into an unfinished beautiful, delicious, crisp mound of home-fries whose pungent odor Remo could taste and even chew.

'Think he's going to win?'

'Nah. He's a long shot, but we got a good deal and we can survive the loss. The international needs us as much as we need them. You're voting for Jethro.'

'According to the bylaws,' said Remo, watching a bacon crisp float in a golden yellow pool of yolk, 'I am obliged to cast my vote independently, free of any reward or pressure, a free honest vote.'

'You go talking like that, you're gonna get us all laughed out of the convention, Remo. Now my deal was only to get you in. Not get us ruined. Don't embarrass us with silly talk like that. That's all. Don't embarrass us. We got enough problems without us trying to pass off Bo Peep as a union official. We made a deal and that's it.'

'That's it,' said Stanziani and Barbetta in unison. 'That's it.'

'Right,' said Bludner agreeing with those who agreed with him.

'You going to eat the leftover potatoes?' Remo asked Bludner.

'No. You want 'em?'

'He doesn't,' said Chiun.

'Well, you guys must be excited about your new union building, it going up so quickly and all that,' said Remo.

'New?' Bludner looked puzzled.

'Just outside this city. A beautiful building. I guess I should call it *our* building now.'

'We ain't got no new building near Chicago. We got our headquarters in Washington. The capital.'

'I see,' said Remo. 'When do I meet Jethro?'

'You'll meet him. You'd probably even like him. He's kind of, don't take offense, like you in some ways.'

'Lucky guy,' said Remo. He smiled at the frowns on the faces of Barbetta and Stanziani.

Bludner outlined the convention program. 'There's a reception tomorrow night after the election. Today, there's the dedication, the convocation, and the reading of last year's minutes. That don't count. You don't have to go. Tomorrow is the nominations and the voting. To that, you gotta go. You vote Jethro. You'll get a button and all that crap. Jethro.'

The waiter returned with a tray. Remo first smelled the rich chocolate fudge, then the aroma of cherry preserves, tangy and pungent. The whipped cream quivered in a silver bowl, a billowing white mountain of sweetness. The nuts were a rich, oily paste. The cinnamon Danish were round and light. Remo grabbed the metal leg of the table. The leg would support *him* as well as the table. He squeezed.

Chiun muttered a Korean word that Remo recognized as 'dog droppings.'

Bludner carefully unspun the round string of cinnamon Danish from a wheel to a long strip. Then he mixed the chocolate fudge with part of the cherry preserve and blended in the nut paste. He coated the inside of the unwound Danish with the reddish-brown sweetness and pushed the bulging pastry back close to its original form. Then he coated the top with the oozing cherry-chocolate paste. Little nut fragments made specks of small rises in the cherry chocolate. Bludner formed three pastries in this fashion and licked the spoon with which he made the paste.

Then he topped the cherry-chocolate mounds with scoops of the fluffy whipped cream, forming it into delicate, sweet mountains. On top of that, Bludner carefully placed cherries. They sank into the whipped cream mountains, tangy red balls in a rise of white.

Suddenly the table jerked. The Dawn Danishes quivered but stayed intact. Remo withdrew his hand from the table leg. In his passion he had cracked it.

'Let us go to our hotel rooms,' said Chiun. 'I cannot watch people degrade their stomachs in such a fashion.'

'In a minute, Chiun,' said Remo. If he knew it would not harm him, Remo for that Dawn Danish would have betrayed any trust in his life. The organization. The country. His mother and father if he had known them. Children if he had had them. And Chiun with a high hurrah.

'You're going to eat it now?' said Remo.

'Yeah,' said Bludner. 'I can make another.'

'No. That's all right,' said Remo. 'Let me watch you.'

Bludner served his men, and then with a fork cut a small triangular wedge and raised it to his mouth. A cherry peeked out of the side of the whipped cream, and appeared to fall. Remo watched the pastry, cherry-chocolate paste, whipped cream and cherries disappear into Bludner's mouth.

'Arghhh,' said Remo.

'If you are hungry, eat good food,' said Chiun and tore some petals from the table daisies. Remo cut them in midair with his fingertips, knowing that the men would not even see his hands move.

Remo got his union card, delegate badge, and Jethro hat from Bludner and returned to his room with Chiun.

The bellboys were bringing in Chiun's large, lacquered trunks. They were told to set up the television device first. The device could be attached to any normal set. But Chiun had had his own set shipped with the device. Once in a Washington motel the television set had faulty wiring and Chiun had missed fifteen minutes of Dr. Lawrence Walters, Psychiatrist. Remo was not sure how a person could miss a segment because nothing ever happened. He had watched the show on two occasions exactly a year apart, and had had no trouble with the continuity.

Chiun saw it differently and had refused to speak to Remo for a week, Remo being the only one who would mind not being spoken to by him.

The television was set up and tuned to a lady's show. Dr. Lawrence Walters would be on in half an hour, followed by 'As the Planet Revolves,' 'Edge of Dawn,' Return to Drury Village.' There was a half hour for exercises. Chiun worked Remo on the fall advance, a basic step that Chiun said was learned anew each time a student improved. Remo thought this absurd when he first mastered the step, but then as he progressed in the discipline, he came to understand that just the simple act of falling and then moving forward had many varied and subtle ramifications.

Remo worked hands, torso, and neck; then hips, thighs, and feet; and finally, as he had done every day since the burns of the electric chair on his hands, feet, and forehead had healed, every day for the last eight years, Remo who had been known as Remo Williams when he was alive and had a different face, and when he was a policeman who had suddenly found himself charged with a murder he did not commit, and gone to the chair when no policeman had gone to the chair for more than sixty years and when there was even talk of the death penalty being abolished—Remo, now Remo Jones, worked on his breathing.

He breathed as few men did, straining his lungs, pushing them to painful limits, imperceptibly farther each day, forcing his bloodstream to make greater and greater use of less oxygen, attuning his very nerve cells to a new consciousness.

He was in a sweat when he finished. He showered, shaved, and donned a double-breasted gray suit with striped tie and shirt. Remembering how Bludner and his men looked, he took off the tie.

'I'm going to the convention, Chiun. What am I having for lunch?'

'A Dawn Danish,' said Chiun laughing.

'Don't you push me, you sonuvabitch.'

'A Dawn Danish,' said Chiun, chuckling again. 'Who could eat that?'

'I'll smash that TV. I will, Chiun. What can I have?'

'Rice and water and three ounces of raw fish. Not cod or halibut. Don't eat the scales.'

'I'm not going to eat the frigging scales, for Chrissakes.'

'Anyone who would eat a Dawn Danish would eat a fish scale,' said Chiun. 'Heh, heh.'

'Heh, heh. I hope they discontinue "As the Planet Revolves." '

Remo arrived at the convention early, as he knew Bludner would. The opening ceremonies were usually attended only by a few wives, a couple of delegates, the incumbent president and his officers. A rabbi, priest and minister offered prayers. Somehow the rabbi got unionism to relate to a greater need for more charities, the priest connected unionism with sex, and the minister alluded to unionism as the social action of its day. Nobody talked much about God.

Remo spoke to a few delegates. They knew nothing about a new building just outside of Chicago. They asked Remo how things were in New York City.

'Rolling,' said Remo. They didn't think that was funny.

'How's Abe?' one asked.

'Good. Good. A real stand-up guy.'

'Yeah. He's a stand-up guy. How's Tony and Paul?'

'Great. Great. They'll be here.'

'Billy Donescu?'

'He's fine. He's not coming.'

'I know he's not coming,' said the delegate. 'He's been dead five years. Now, who the hell are you? You ain't no driver.'

'Don't bother me with that nonsense,' said Remo. 'I'm a driver in spirit.'

The delegate called over a man known as the sergeant at arms. The sergeant at arms called over two guards. The two guards called over five more, and Remo was escorted to the entrance. But at the entrance a funny thing happened. The guards stumbled with painful groin injuries, the sergeant at arms suffered a broken collarbone, and the delegates were looking for fallen teeth. Remo strode back to the center of the Convention Hall, whistling pleasantly.

'He's for real,' said one delegate. 'He don't sound it but he's for real. Abe has got himself a real boy this time.'

The news—really important news in the drivers' union travels from mouth to mouth—reached Abe 'Crowbar' Bludner, as he was preparing for the real convention business in the afternoon. It came in the form of a delegate from Louisiana. A redheaded, rawboned man with a heavy drawl, for whom Abe had done favors from time to time.

'You are some sweetheart,' said the Southerner with a grin. 'You are some real, real sweetheart. Whoowee.'

'What's up?' asked Bludner, opening his collar two buttons.

'Yo' new business agent. Ain't he a what fo'?'

Abe Bludner felt a sudden stretching of his throat. He cleared it.

'Remo Jones? He went to the convention alone?'

'Y'all can bet yo danged mule,' said the Southern delegate.

Just like these Southerners, thought Bludner, to castrate

a defenseless animal. Well, at least they weren't doing it to minority groups anymore.

'Hold on,' said Bludner. 'He's all right. A little bit funny, but look. So's Gene Jethro, you know. And every man has a right to act his own way. He's okay.'

'Ah know. That son of a gull lizard is one peck o' nails,' said the Southern delegate.

'You mean he's got a set of kishkas,' said Bludner.

'What're kishkas?'

'What's a peck o' nails?'

'Hard. Real hard.'

'Yeah. That's what a kishka is, too, I guess.'

'But ah ain't seen nuthin like ah heard he is. Whoo-wee. Is that man a peck o' nails.'

Bludner looked at the other delegate surprised.

'Remo Jones? Our business agent?'

'Right.'

'Hey Tony, Paul. Did you hear that?'

'Yeah, we heard,' they called out from an adjoining bedroom where they were playing gin.

'What do you know?' said Abe 'Crowbar' Bludner. 'What do you know?'

'You guys from Local 529 are real stand-up guys,' said the Southern delegate. 'Real stand-up.'

'You gotta be,' said Abe 'Crowbar' Bludner. 'You gotta be.'

SIX

Other people from Remo's organization were at the convention. But he was the only one who knew his employer. Other people throughout the country sent their messages to destinations of which they knew not. Other hands and other eyes worked to stem the events which would lead to a union so powerful that a nation would be at its mercy. Moment by moment the reports, all ending at the desk of a man called Harold Smith, director of a sanitarium in Rye, New York, became worse. The plan to control American transportation seemed invincible.

A union clerk, preparing the giant electrical boards in convention hall for the coming vote, noted that everything appeared to be running smoothly. No attempts to tamper with the machinery, no offers of bribes, no sudden influx of repairmen with strange credentials. Just a normal, routine, dull checking-out of the equipment.

From a pay phone, he transmitted this information to a person he believed was doing a book on the union movement. Why the person should want immediate information the moment certain things happened, the clerk did not bother to ask. The money was regular, and since it came in envelopes, it was not taxable.

A vice-president of an airline company routinely phoned his business adviser. The adviser was obviously CIA or something like that, but such matters were not the executive's concern. He had risen fast with the help of this adviser—it was a small enough price to pay for a career. The president of his company was willing to make a deal for some strange upcoming contract that none of the other executives knew about. His airline would be the only one allowed to operate for an entire month if it gave the union everything it wanted. The airline had purchased extra planes for this planned overload of passengers. Strange, that any union could guarantee that. Stranger still was that the adviser had asked for just that kind of information recently.

An accountant in Duluth, Minnesota, got angry with his employer, the Joint Council of the Brotherhood of Railroad Workmen.

'You can't just say "contribution to unionism." You've got to list which union. If it is not called the Brotherhood of Railroad Workmen, then, gentlemen, it is not your union, and I cannot put it in the books that way. I'm sorry. But should there be an audit of these books, if I did what you ask, I would be spending considerable time behind bars. Let alone losing my practice.'

The accountant assured his clients, however, that he could proceed without listing the expenditures until the end of the fiscal year.

'That's all right. That's fine,' said the president of the joint council. 'We'll only need a week at the outside.'

The accountant gave the books and records of the recent money transfers to his secretary to put into the office safe. This she did, but only after she had made a photocopy for the lovely person at the big department store who liked to collect things like this. He was so nice, that person, he had given her a special charge account. Extended time payments. Nothing down and one percent a year for two years, and the store would make up the difference. The account would be allowed to jump at various very pleasant times. Like when one of their clients was engaged in an oil swindle with a Wall Street stock brokerage firm. That paid for the dinette, the playroom, and the new color TV. What she wanted most now was a new kitchen. She should get it. The man at the department store had specifically asked for this information. Maybe a new washer-dryer, too. Although she already had two of those.

The lovely person at the department store was thrilled with the photocopies of the documents, so thrilled that he suggested the secretary redecorate her living room. He dialed a special number and surrendered the copy of the documents to his contact, a man he believed was in the FBI. The man was in the FBI, having been transferred to special assignment four years ago. He gave the documents immediately to an undercover office where a woman received them. She knew she wasn't working for the FBI. She was working on a secret mission for the State Department. She was one of their top programmers. She punched the information into the terminal in her office. She had never been able to generate any feedback to see if she were correct. But that was all right. That was a safety device always used by secret operations so that unauthorized personnel would not have access to the information. Only those special people in Washington would be able to get the information from State Department computers.

The information did not go to the State Department, however. The lines led to a sanitarium in Rye, New York, called Folcroft. There, another computer expert supervised the input. Like many computer programmers, he was not sure where the information fit or even how it fit. But if everything worked right, and he was sure it was working right, the gigantic study on the effect of the economy on national health would most certainly prove a momentous and significent report.

Only one terminal could draw feedback from the Folcroft computers and that was in the office of Dr. Harold Smith, director of the sanitarium and director of the study.

Under the oak veneer of his desk was a control panel. There was also a slot for a computer printout. This printout did not drop into a basket, but was fed directly into an electric disposal device passing for only nine inches under a visible glass panel, visible when the veneer slid away to reveal the controls.

The panel was open now and Dr. Smith's lemon face was even more bitter than usual. He watched the green paper with the square typing move like a long green river under the reading glass from computer terminal to electric disposal. He could signal a return of any information, but he could not hold it in his hands.

Outside, through the one-way glass behind him, the Long Island Sound lapped at the shores, a dark body extending into the Atlantic. People had crossed this ocean to establish a new land, a land of law, a land of justice, a land where a piece of paper protected poor and rich alike. And that piece of paper did not work. And justice was a sometime thing. But the hope was left. The hope was coming out of this computer terminal: these times would pass, and one day, without it ever having been known to anyone but those whose lives were dedicated to its secrecy, each President who passed the secret to his successor, the organization would just dissolve. Having not existed, it would not exist.

That was why Dr. Smith could not hold the paper in his hands. Evidence could not be allowed to exist. Like the organization, it would be secret for a few moments in time, then disappear.

Smith read the flowing printout and his face became more bitter with each line.

'Damn,' he said, and spun his swivel chair from the machine to look out on Long Island Sound in the darkness of night. A few boats blinked off shore. Smith drummed his fingers on the leather arm of the swivel chair.

'Damn,' he said again. He watched the lights a moment, then reran the printout. It was, of course, the same. Nothing had changed, and as he realized that he could not alter the inevitable conclusion, his mind wandered to the time when there was no glass paneling over the printout and he could pick it up and file it in a locked drawer.

One of the sheets—accidentally, despite all precautions

—had gotten mixed with the normal sanitarium work, and his brightest assistant, who had nothing whatever to do with the real work of the organization, just the medical cover, had discovered it. That had set him off on a little puzzle. And one day he happily told Dr. Smith he knew what Folcroft really did. He was smiling as he outlined a function all too close to the way CURE really operated.

'Very interesting,' Dr. Smith had said smiling. 'What do others think?'

'What others?' said the assistant.

'You know. One man couldn't figure all this out.'

'I most certainly did,' beamed the assistant. 'I know you, sir, and I know you are an honorable man, and you wouldn't be involved in anything illegal or immoral. So I figured what you were doing must be for a good cause. And I didn't want to hurt the cause, so I kept it strictly to myself. Besides, it was more fun that way. This was a most interesting problem.'

'I commend you,' said Dr. Smith. 'Well, I guess our secret's safe with you.'

'It most certainly is, sir. And good luck in your good work.'

'Thank you,' said Dr. Smith. 'The work is very trying. I'm leaving on vacation in about a half hour. The coast, Malibu beach.'

'I was born there.'

'Oh, were you?'

'Yes. Didn't you read my application? Born there twenty-six years ago this August. I can still smell the Pacific. You know it breathes easier than the Atlantic.'

'Then come with me,' Dr. Smith said with sudden joy. 'Come. We'll both go. I won't take "no" for an answer. I want you to meet my nephew, Remo.'

And that was when the glass was installed on the print-out mechanism designed to clean the machine whether Dr. Smith pressed the button or not. He hated what he had to do, hated what he did to his luckless assistant, hated the very cunning and duplicity which ran counter to his nature. It was not so difficult, when a former employee of another government agency attempted to blackmail CURE. That had a moral justification. But what was Dr. Braithwait's crime? That he was an internist? That he was closer to death than another internist of his caliber? What was the young assistant's crime? That he was clever. That he was honest and meant well, and that if he had wished the organization evil and given the information to the *New York Times*, he would be alive today? Was that his crime, punishable by death?

Smith turned off the terminal and watched the electric disposal pull the last few paragraphs into its blades. Woodpulp returned to woodpulp, with its interim existence as a communication form gone forever.

He looked out at the Sound, then checked his watch. Remo would be phoning in five hours and twelve minutes, when the juxtaposition of the special circuits was right. Not enough time to go home and sleep. Better to sleep here in the chair. Perhaps there would be new information in the morning, and he would not have to tell Remo what at this point he must tell him. Perhaps the problem-solving team, which worked with symbols, would come up with a different answer. After all, they were at Folcroft as a human check on a mechanical function.

They were never informed as to what the symbols really meant, of course, but they had often produced creative ideas—ideas beyond the capability of the computer—never knowing how these management theory ideas would be translated into action.

Smith closed his eyes. Yes, maybe the problem-solving team would come up with a different solution.

Long Island Sound was gray-blue and white, sparkling in the sun, when Smith awoke. It was 8 A.M.; the problem-solving team would have its overnight report in a few minutes. He had asked for it early. The buzzer was ringing on his desk. He pushed intercom.

'Yes?' he said.

'We got it, sir,' came the voice.

'Come on in.' said Smith. He pressed another button and the large oak door silently unlocked. As the door opened, the computer panel shut automatically, catching Smith's elbow and giving him a nasty pain.

'Are you all right, sir?' asked the member of the problem-solving team. He was in his late thirties and worry showed very well on his face.

'No. No. I'm all right,' said Dr. Smith grimacing. 'What do you have?'

'Well, sir. According to the relationships of all the groups in this contract to buy and sell grain, we get, considering all variables, a breakdown in the bargaining process.'

'I see,' said Dr. Smith.

'No way around it, sir. If there is no other major basic staple on the market, the person who represents the multitude of heretofore loosely connected grainsellers, has got a gun at the buyer's head. He doesn't ask for a price, he sets it?'

'There's no other way around it?'

'No. Not offhand. But you see, with the increasing price there will be a fall in demand and the price will settle. Settle high, but settle.'

'And what if the grain-seller doesn't want to sell?'

'That's absurd, sir. He's got to want to sell. Otherwise, why corner the market? That's the purpose, isn't it?'

'Yes. I guess so. Thank you. Thank you.'

'Glad to be of help.'

'You have been, thank you.'

When the man left the office, Dr. Smith slammed the arm of his chair again.

'Damn. Damn. Damn.'

Remo's call came through at 8.15.

'Remo?' said Dr. Smith.

'No. Candace Bergen,' came Remo's voice.

'I'm glad you're in fine spirits. You can move to the next stage now. It looks as though we are going to the extreme plan.'

'The one you said you were sure we wouldn't have to use?'

'That's right.'

'Why don't you just bomb the convention hall and have done with it?'

'I am in no mood for your humor now, young man. No mood at all.'

'Look. Feed this into your computers. I'm not going to do it. Work out something else. Or I will.'

'Remo. This is a hard, hard thing for me to ask. But you must prepare for the extreme plan. There just isn't anyone else.'

'Then there isn't anyone else.'

'You will do it.'

'As a matter of fact, I won't. As a matter of fact, since I recovered from that little incident, I have been depressed as I have never been depressed before. But that's a human emotion and you wouldn't understand that. I am a human being, you sonuvabitch. Do you hear that. I am a human being.'

The receiver clicked dead. It had been hung up in Chicago. Dr. Smith drummed his fingers on the chair arm. It had sounded foreboding, but it was really not. Remo would do what he would have to do. There was no way he could *not* carry out his function, any more than he could eat a hamburger laced with monosodium glutamate.

SEVEN

The convention buzzed and roared and yelled and clapped and paraded up and down the aisles for candidates, beer, and washrooms, the last receiving less vocal but more sincere enthusiasm. There were three nominations for president of the International Brotherhood of Drivers at convention hall, and after each name, the delegates flooded the center aisle, placards aloft, as if it were a political convention. They went onto a frenzy of screaming, as though victory depended upon decibel instead of delegate count.

When Jethro's name went into nomination, Abe 'Crowbar' Bludner grabbed a two-by-four with a poster stapled to it and led the local delegates and the New York City joint council delegates into the stream of driver delegates demonstrating for the young man from Nashville. Remo did not rise with the delegation. He did not move. He crossed a leg and rested his chin on his hand.

This quiet meditation in a section of empty seats stood out like Stations of the Cross at an orgy. It did not go unnoticed. Gene Jethro, beaming from the platform and waving to supporters, said over his shoulder to Negronski:

'Who's that?'

'That's the guy who did the job on the sergeant of arms, guards, and the Arizona delegates.'

'So that's him,' said Jethro. 'When you can get to him unnoticed, tell him I want to see him.'

All this did Gene Jethro say while his face to the crowd

beamed happy enthusiasm. He noticed the false lack of concern of his opponent's face and gave him an extra Gene Jethro grin, this one broader, fuller.

The opponent grinned back.

'I'm gonna run you out of the union,' yelled the opponent, his face apparent joy.

'You're through, old man,' Jethro yelled back, his face even more an explosion of joy and happiness. 'You're dead. Let the dead bury the dead.'

From the floor it looked like a friendly interchange between two friendly rivals. Remo did not watch it. He felt the yelling, felt the movement, felt the excitement, but he did not watch it or listen to it. He thought about himself and knew he had been lying to himself for the past few years. It took a simple, plain, American hamburger, which millions of people ate and he could not, to show him up, to strip him of years of self-deception.

When he had first consented to work for the organization, he had entertained the thought of one day going on assignment and keeping on going. He was always going to quit next month or the month after that. A few times he was going to take the walk in the afternoon.

And these afternoons were followed by months which became years, and years. And each day, the training progressed. Each day Chiun had worked on his mind, and his mind had worked on his body. And he had not noticed the change. He knew that he was a little bit different—a little bit faster than boxers, a little bit stronger than weightlifters, and a little bit more shifty than running backs—and that his body was a little bit more attuned than the best in most of the rest of the world. But he had thought, and had fiercely supported this thought, that he was not really different.

He had believed that some day he might have a family, a home, and maybe even a nine-to-five job somewhere. And if he watched himself carefully, perhaps, although this was doubtful, just perhaps he would have ten or fifteen years before someone from the organization would knock on his door and put a bullet in his face. (If it were a successor, it would be a hand in the face.)

Ten or fifteen years of belonging, of existing, of having people need you in their lives, and of you needing them. The only person he cared about now would kill him on orders—because that was the business. And what bothered Remo now was that he knew he, too, on orders, would kill Chiun—because that was the business. He would do it and, incidentally, find out if he could take the Master of Sinanju, his teacher.

And for knowing that he would do this, he hated himself to his very guts. He was no different from the other assassins of Sinanju except for the color of his skin. and that, he knew, was no difference at all.

The delegates vented their spontaneous joy to the full twenty minutes, as scheduled, and returned, yelling and screaming, to their seats. The New York delegation brushed past Remo and he hardly noticed them. Bludner sat down next to him and handed him the placard. Remo took it without looking.

'You okay, kid?' asked Bludner.

But Remo did not answer. He looked up at the big banner stretched across the roof of the arena, and he automatically thought of the wind currents and the months of becoming attuned to air as a cushion, as a force, as an obstacle and an ally. This thinking was so automatic that he detested it. His mind was no longer his own. Why should he be surprised that his body reacted so independently of his wishes? Why should he be surprised that eating a hamburger containing monosodium glutamate, something a child could do, would be impossible for him? He knew now why he had yelled at Smith, why he had yelled that he was a human being. He had to yell it. Lies always require more energy.

Remo watched the air currents work on the banner. Maybe a beam falling on the speaker's platform, provided it could be guided to strike one end first.... He stood up to check the rows of seats on the platform. If it hit right, just right, it could take the first two rows. That would leave the third row free.

'Abe, give me an agenda,' Remo said.

'How come you're suddenly interested in this thing, kid?'

'I am. I am. Give me an agenda.'

'Hey, Tony. Give the kid an agenda,' Bludner called out.

A folder with the brotherhood's emblem was passed down the row.

'Thanks,' said Remo not taking his eyes off the platform. He opened the agenda and went through the program for Wednesday: acceptance speech, proposed amendment to the bylaws, an address by a senator from Missouri. No good. Thursday: a tribute to drivers' wives, a speech by the president of the American Legion, a vote on the proposed amendment. No good.

Friday: speeches by the president of the Brotherhood of Railroad Workmen, president of the International Stevedores Association, president of the Airline Pilots Association, and the final address—by the secretary of labor. Beautiful.

'Hey, Abe, when people are scheduled to speak, do they come on just when they speak or do they sit there through the whole thing?'

'They gotta sit through the whole thing, kid,' said Bludner. 'Why do you ask?'

'I don't know. It just seems boring, you know.'

'Kid, I didn't like beg you to come to this thing.'

'I know. I know. But just sitting there in the third row, behind two rows of heads, waiting to give your speech, sounds boring.'

'They don't sit in the third row, kid. They sit up front. The speechmakers are always some kind of guest of honor. I thought I'd get someone with smarts, kid. You're pretty, well, I don't mean to be insulting, pretty thick.'

'Yeah, I guess so,' said Remo, sitting down. The banner flapped, then ruffled, then dropped and remained still for a moment before flapping again. The beam undoubtedly was bolted, and since the lights were dropped from the ceiling, a person maneuvering along the lattice of the ceiling might not be seen. If the secretary of labor were making his speech, the worst he would suffer would be a broken back.

On Friday, before the final meeting, Remo would work his way to that beam. He would loosen it in such a way that vibrations against the supporting beams would loosen it, like a balanced matchstick, only this matchstick weighed thousands of pounds.

Remo gauged the wind currents. While they could not affect so heavy an object to a great degree, they could affect it enough. No. He could not count on it swinging from its other joining. He would have to take off one end and leave the other by a thread of a rivet. Now would the currents working on this Goliath of a beam set vibrations to loosen it before its time? Remo peered at the banner and watched a balloon float up to the ceiling. No. Not enough currents. That would be workable.

He looked again at the platform on which the union leaders would sit, the key man in turning off America's vital arteries. Well, if Bludner weren't right about the seating, he would have to rearrange himself.

It was an extreme move, this mass killing, and Remo deemed it risky, both in the purpose of the organization and the execution of it. The news of it would be just too big. There would be too strong an investigation. The investigation might even uncover the organization. But more than that it was the way Smith had explained the operation.

For anyone to get control of transportation, as this projected superunion planned to do, would mean a total rupture of the American economy and ultimately the American way of life. The rising cost of transportation would be passed on where it was always passed on. To the little consumer. Meat, vegetables, and milk, already too high, would rise beyond—way beyond—the pockets of the once best-fed people on earth. Welfare recipients and people on fixed incomes would be reduced to the diet of a poverty-stricken nation. In response to these rising prices, due in large part to the rising costs of transportation, wages would have to rise. An inflation such as the nation had never before known would ensue. People would bring their American dollars to the supermarket in shopping carts and carry their food home in their purses. During a strike of this superunion, unemployment would be worse than it was in the depression of the thirties. This superunion would kill the nation, if the nation did not enact laws killing the union first. But if that were to happen, then the union movement in America, which had helped give the worker respect as a human being, would also be doomed.

Weighed in the balance against this were the lives of four union leaders. Unless another plan were evolved, they must die. Remo focused on the beam.

'Hey, Abe,' he said.

'Yeah, kid.'

'Why don't you think Jethro is going to win? Who's going to stop him?'

'New England, for one. They got a whole bloc. And this guy McCulloch who leads it is anti-Jethro. Hates his guts. Tried to lean on me to switch. I wouldn't. But McCulloch is gonna swing it against Jethro. Whoever seems to be winning other than Jethro is gonna get McCulloch and New England. Too much to stop.'

Remo looked around the convention hall.

'Point him out to me.'

Without getting up, Bludner pointed, forward right, ostensibly through the wide, white-shirted back of the man just in front.

'About twenty rows that way, in the Massachusetts, Connecticut, Maine, New Hampshire, and Vermont sections. They're all lumped together. You won't be able to see his head, but you'll see guys going in and out of the aisles towards one spot, leaning down to talk and stuff. In that spot will be a guy six-foot-four, red hair, a good 280, maybe 300 pounds. That's McCulloch.'

Remo stood on his chair but could not see the action described.

'I don't see any one special spot guys are going to,' he said.

'It's there. It's there. Look.' said Bludner.

'Hey, siddown,' came a voice from behind Remo, 'I can't see.'

Remo peered twenty rows ahead, saw the New England state signs, but no one person was the center of attention.

'Hey, buddy. I asked you nice. Now will you siddown?' came the deep voice.

'Siddown, Remo. You can walk over,' said Bludner. 'And you, leave the kid alone. He'll sit down in a second.'

A ball of a man in white sports shirt and trousers that looked like sheeting for a zeppelin wended his way down the Massachusetts row. Maybe he was going to stop to talk.

'Hey buddy. How about it?' came the voice, and Remo felt a tap on his backside. He caught the hand with his own, splitting the knuckle joints. He wasn't too interested in what was going on behind him. Up front the ball of a man was about to speak to someone. He was leaning over. No. He was sitting down. Damn. Where the hell was McCulloch? He'd have to go over to the delegation. Remo stepped down from his seat. Bludner was looking at him, funny. A tall rock of a man behind him was clutching his right hand with his left as though cutting off blood and nerves to his knuckles. His face was agony. He jumped from one foot to another. Remo looked at the hand. The knuckles. Someone had split the knuckles. That must be the man who had touched him on the backside. Of course, that was he.

'Put some cold water on it,' said Remo. He excused himself to Bludner, whose large mouth hung open.

'Don't mess wit da kid,' said Bludner. 'Don't mess wit him.'

Rembo wended his way to the Massachusetts delegation. He looked for McCulloch. He called for McCulloch. He even insulted McCulloch. But no McCulloch.

'Hey, where the hell is McCulloch?' asked Remo.

The fat man he had seen move through the row yelled back:

'Who wants to know?'

'Remo Jones. New York delegate.'

'He ain't here.'

'Where is he?'

'He's gone.'

'Is that a Jethro button I see?' said Remo.

'No. It's a Wendell Willkie button.'

'You're pretty smart for someone who's illiterate,' said Remo, lost for a more effective insult.

'I'm not illustrated,' yelled the man. 'You're illustrated. Faghead.'

So much for a dialogue on union politics.

Bludner found the information about the button very interesting. He listened to how nobody would say where McCulloch was; he saw how New England people were now wearing Jethro buttons.

'You know I could have sworn I saw some New Englanders in that Jethro demonstration,' he said. He signaled for the microphone at the end of the row. He jumped up on two chairs to a cracking sound of the wood. He waved an arm above his head.

'Point of order,' he yelled. 'Mr. Chairman. Point of order. The New York delegation of joint councils and locals wishes to make a point of order.'

The chair recognized the brother delegate from New York City.

'Mr. Chairman, brothers from all the states, fellow drivers. It is a disgrace. It is an outrage. It is an injustice,' boomed Abe 'Crowbar' Bludner, president of Local 529, New York City. 'That the picture of one of the greatest union men ever to stand up for the rights of working men is not prominently displayed at this convention. I am talking about the finest, stand-up, all around wonderful guy in the entire International Brotherhood of Drivers. Eugene V. Jethro, the next president of the international...'

Bludner's voice was drowned in cheers, which precipitated another frenzied demonstration. The chairman banged his gavel, calling the New York delegation and the demonstration out of order, but with little effect.

Abe Bludner sat down proudly, amid the chaos he had instigated.

'Thanks for the info, kid,' he said.

But Remo hardly heard him. He was wondering whether the beam upon which the banner fluttered was new or was installed when the convention hall was built. It made a difference if you were going to drop it on someone's head.

EIGHT

Three brass bands blared rock hits six months old. Portly women with lacquered hair and just as stiff faces held the arms of their bulky husbands in black tuxedoes, white formal shirts and black bowties. Here and there someone wore a checkered tux. Here and there a woman wore a black sheath. Here and there people were not middle aged and middle class and middle bored. But only here and there.

The Gene Jethro victory celebration was a middle-class, husband and wife party that, with the help of a few horns and a few hats, could have substituted for countless New Year's Eve parties across America.

For the drivers were family men, and so were their union delegates. Men with homes and cars and television sets and all the worries and comforts of a working class unique in the history of man. No other nation had ever given the worker so much. And in no other nation had the worker taken so much. In return for this hard-won largesse, these workers had put a man on the moon and had won wars on two oceans simultaneously. No other nation had done that either. Some workers would steal a case of whisky from a truckload. A small, very small, fraction would help a hijack. But the flag flew at all conventions, and if you were in trouble, these were the men who would stand by you. They put food on their tables, dresses on their wives, and hands on their hearts when 'The Star-Spangled Banner' was played.

Few of them, if any, could figure out how a Gene

Jethro type had won their presidency. A few privately confessed, but only to close friends, that if they thought he was going to win it, they would have voted for someone else. On the third rye and ginger or bourbon on the rocks, the future of the International Brotherhood of Drivers brightened immeasurably. Jethro had won the presidency. That took brains. He had made good deals. That took brains. He had good press. That took brains. So he talked a bit funny and dressed funny. So what? Didn't Joe Namath act kind of faggy? But look at him on a football field. This mood of hopefulness lasted until Gene Jethro, the youngest president in the history of the drivers union, appeared with his mistress at the victory celebration in the Sheraton Park ballroom.

The initial cheers, an automatic response to new power and victory, died on the lips of the driver delegates. It was the wives who stopped cheering first. Gene Jethro was bad enough. He wore a blue velvet one-piece jump suit opened to the navel.

His young, blond mistress's dress was not opened to the navel. It was open *from* it. With a see-through fishnet over bare flesh. Her blond hair flowed gloriously long as she blew kisses to the delegates.

Wives nudged husbands. Some with sharp elbows. Others with icy stares. One woman erased her husband's smile with a champagne cocktail she had been nursing all evening.

'Disgraceful,' said one.

'I thought he would at least marry her once he became president,' said another.

'I don't believe it,' said another.

It was not that these men or their wives were without natural reproductive drives. Sex, however, was not for mixed company, 'mixed' being husband and wife. Almost all the men had their outside arrangements even if it were a local prostitute twice a month. For the women, there were long talks with their girl friends and chocolate candy substitutes. But to bring something like this to a mixed affair—well, that was too much. It just wasn't done.

'Your president,' snarled Mrs. Sigmund Negronski to her husband. 'Your president and his, his tramp. I don't know what sort of dirty minds have taken over the drivers, but let me tell you, Siggy, it will be a cold day in August before you'll ever lay one of your filthy hands on me.'

Negronski shrugged. It was not exactly the worst threat in the world. What was bad about it was that his wife would stop talking to him also, as though the two things went together.

Mrs. Abe Bludner saw the thin, vital blossoming body in the fishnet and immediately felt depressed, so depressed that she stuffed another hors d'oeuvre into her mouth. Having felt sufficiently depressed with her age and weight, she reminded her husband of how he had left her stranded on the Narragansett Parkway in 1942 and how she should have known back then, back in 1942, left all alone in the family car, that he would do such a thing as vote for that exhibitionist who should be in jail. Jail was for people who exposed themselves. Forgiveness was for people who broke other people's heads with crowbars. At least that wasn't dirty.

Mrs. Rocco Pigarello looked at the man her husband had voted for, looked at the woman he was with, and gently tapped her husband's giant girth. When he turned his face to her, she spit.

The three brass bands emitted trumpet and drum salutes, and Gene Jethro grabbed one of the microphones. A lone clapper accentuated the silence.

'Hi there, dudes,' said Gene Jethro.

Silence.

'I'm glad you've come here to help me celebrate a victory, not only for the drivers of America, but for the people of America. We're going to do some great things together. Meaningful things. And I just want to thank you all.'

A few claps.

'But I don't think there is anything as meaningful as our own new minimum wage. Airline pilots make well over $30,000 a year base. And they drive planes. Dock-workers, if they work full time all year, can bring home $18,000 a year. If one of our drivers earns $15,000 a year, he's doing all right. Well, that's not all right with me. I don't see the difference between a man who hauls freight on the ground and a man who hauls freight off a ship. I don't see the difference between a man who drives a truck on a road and a man who drives an airplane in the sky.

'Too long have we been taken for granted. Too long has a couple of hundred a week been considered adequate base pay for our union members. Too long have our men come home weary and tired and broken of body and mind for a paltry two hundred a week, if they make that.'

Jethro paused to allow his indignation to infect his audience.

'You tell 'em, Geney baby,' yelled one of the women. 'Give 'em hell.'

'We are the biggest and strongest single transportation union in the country. In the world.'

Cheers filled the ballroom. Loud whistles rent the air. Hands beat together in a growling, surging applause.

Gene Jethro raised his hands to quiet his audience.

'They tell me that a driver isn't worth $25,000 a year.'

Gasps. Disbelief. Some applause.

'But I'm going to tell them that if you want to eat, if you want to drink milk or soda or anything else, if you want your television sets or new cars, you're gonna pay your drivers $25,000 a year. And these drivers are going to pay their union representatives the kind of salaries that an executive representing $25,000-a-year men deserves. I'm talking $100,000 for business agents. I'm talking $110,000 for recording secretaries. I'm talking $115,000 for vice-presidents and $125,000 a year for presidents of locals.'

Again silence. The figures were beautiful, but unbelievable.

'Now many of you think these figures are too high. Many of you think we can never get that much. Many of you figure that's a nice promise but a weak reality. But let me ask you now. Whoever thought I would become president of this union? Raise your hand. Go ahead. Raise your hand. You're full of shit, Siggy, and you told me just yesterday you thought we were going to jail.'

Laughter.

'By this Friday, every one of you will see how we're going to be able to turn this country on and off like a water faucet. By this Friday, you are going to see why the basic salary of a truck driver is going to have to be $25,000 a year if we say so. By this Friday, you will see how I am going to work this thing. I promise you here. I promise you now. I, legally, bindingly, solemnly promise I will resign if every one of you does not see how I am going to work this thing for you. Now that's a promise. And I keep promises.'

Jethro dropped his hands to his sides and stared at his audience. There was a stony silence. Then someone clapped and the house came down. Women rushed to the stage to kiss Jethro's hands. They fought their husbands who were trying to shake the same hands. The bands tried to play along with the enthusiasm but were drowned out by shrieking, yelling drivers and their wives.

'Jethro. Jethro. Jethro,' the crowd began to chant. 'Jethro. Jethro. Jethro.' His girl friend's blouse was ripped off in the melee. But that was all right. You could have seen everything before, anyhow. And besides, maybe that was just one of the new styles.

Jethro gracefully skirted away from his adoring followers after a proper enough time to receive adulation. He signaled for Negronski.

'Siggy,' he said behind a bandstand where hopefully he would be left alone for a moment. 'Why isn't that New York delegate here?'

'I asked him,' said Negronski.

'And?'

'And I don't know. He said something funny, like it doesn't make any difference anymore.'

'Look. He seemed very strange. I'm hearing even stranger things about him. Now, I want him to be at my suite by noon tomorrow, or I do not want him to be at all. Understand. Take Pigarello and the other New England boys with you. Let them get their hands dirty. If Bludner causes you any trouble, let me know first and I'll handle the whole thing. Okay?'

'Bludner ain't going to let you lean on one of his boys.'

'Does Remo Jones look like one of Bludner's boys to you?'

'He's got credentials.'

'I'll take vibrations over ink any day of the week. I don't think Bludner would say "boo" if we nailed this Remo Jones to the front of a tractor trailer and rammed it into the convention hall. I don't think he'd say boo.'

NINE

The piece about Jethro in the Wednesday morning paper was a typical newspaper story. Remo read it to Chiun. The Master of Sinanju, Remo's trainer since he first went to work for the organization, liked newspaper stories. They were almost as pretty as 'Edge of Dawn' or the other shows with good guys and bad guys and dramatic things going to happen which would dramatically change other things, with subtle reasons for things that didn't happen, and with all those wonderful little songs that politicians and militants and labor leaders and association presidents sing.

'Song' was Chiun's word for beautiful speeches. They were judged on thoughts and words alone and not expected to have anything to do with reality. As Chiun had said, truth ruins the really good songs.

'Read,' said Chiun, and lowered himself to lotus position, his robes flowing gently around his frail body.

'Dateline, Chicago,' said Remo. 'Good-bye, beer bellies and roadside diners. Hello, bell bottoms and Consciousness III. The International Brotherhood of Drivers yesterday in a surprise vote chose the young mod Eugene V. Jethro, 26, as its new president.

'The upset came after a bitter, hard-fought, two-month campaign that showed the youthful Jethro to be a master politician with a gentle touch. Said Jethro:

'"I think the day of the strong arm is over. I think the day of the image of the burly driver ready to fight and strike over a bargaining issue has gone with the horse and wagon. We are a new union dedicated to new principles for a new membership. We look to a greater understanding of our relationship to our environment. We will not be turned aside by the old canards of reaction, racism and ruthlessness. Our trucks are headed toward a better total life for ourselves, our families and our neighbors," said Jethro.

'He called the vote a mandate for change. He said America needed an organized transportation front, but did not elaborate.'

Chiun nodded.

'Is there anything on Viet Nam? Those are the prettiest songs,' he asked.

'Another offensive.'

'Read it.'

So Remo read Chiun about the new offensive, and Chiun nodded.

'Why did not your government back the north? You have more money than anyone. Why did you not support the north?'

'Because they're Communist, Chiun.'

'Communist, fascist, democratic, monarchist, loyalist, or falangist. There is only winning. Even you know that. But this is a silly land. And it is time for lunch. Today you may have duck.'

'Roast?'

'Steamed.'

'Oh. Where am I going to get steamed duck?'

'We will steam it here. And I shall add the most flavorful spices.'

'Yeah,' said Remo.

'A three-stone duck,' said Chiun.

'They don't weigh by stones, Chiun. You know that. I'll get a two-and-a-half-pound duck.'

'Three stones,' said Chiun, refusing to be contaminated by Western measurements. And it was time for 'Edge of Dawn.'

Remo was halfway out of the hotel door when a roly-poly fellow with a heavy beard accosted him. He introduced himself as Pigarello. He said Jethro wished to see him. He said Jethro was disturbed that Remo hadn't attended the victory celebration the night before. He said Jethro was a forgiving man. He said Jethro would forgive Remo if he came to see him right now. What could be more important than seeing the new president of the International Brotherhood of Drivers?

'A three-stone duck for steaming,' said Remo.

'Wha?' said the Pig.

'Look. Don't bother me,' said Remo.

Would it be all right if Pigarello walked along?

'Yeah. Yeah. Waddle to your heart's content,' said Remo.

Pigarello knew a shortcut to a duck store.

'Ho, ho, ho,' said Remo to himself. 'That's nice,' said Remo to Pigarello.

'It's through that alley over there,' said Pigarello.

'Ho, ho, ho,' said Remo to himself. 'That alley. Will you come with me?'

Pigarello couldn't. He had to see the new president right away.

'All right. We'll square things later,' said Remo. 'Do you take a regular sized coffin or a hefty?'

'Ho, ho, ho,' laughed Rocco 'the Pig' Pigarello.

'Ho, ho, ho,' thought Remo, waving good-bye to Pigarello and walking casually into the narrow alley, just the width of a tractor trailer. Surprise, surprise, it was a dead end.

Surprise, surprise, the two doors in the alley leading into the surrounding brick buildings were locked. And surprise, surprise, across the street, across the street making its turn forty yards away, was a large, four-axle jobby. A tractor trailer it was, its horse a good fifteen feet high and diesel chugging the house-long shiny metal trailer.

It had to full-turn to come into the alley on a line because otherwise it would never fit. There was no extra room. The truck nosed into the alley, making a fourth side and blocking escape. The large side-view mirrors snapped at the alley entrance and Remo suddenly noticed a real surprise. He had committed the classic mistake of underestimating his enemy.

He had assumed they would use a regular tractor trailer with a regular bumper on the front of the horse. But this was a special vehicle, designed specifically for his death. In front, there was a bumper, but it was painted on. In front there were wheels, but they too were painted on in front of the real moving wheels. In front there were the headlights, but they, too, were painted. That they were false, did not matter. But beneath the painted bumper and between the painted wheels was the large dark space through which Remo had assumed he could easily slip. That was painted on and it could prove fatal for not being there. The false front appeared to be heavy steel, like a bulldozer. The front rode above the oil-slick, concrete alleyway by a foot, clear light under the oncoming steel wall.

A foot might just be enough. The front lowered, chipping the concrete, catching an empty can and sending it hurling over Remo's shoulder. Even the narrow space was gone.

The air was oppressively hot. The walls of the surrounding buildings trembled as the huge truck lumbered further in, like a giant prong in a giant socket. Remo could smell the sickening diesel fuel of the monster pushing the steel wall toward him in the three-sided alley. He looked back at the building to his left. It had a ledge. He could make the ledge, and he broke for it. But looking at the truck and the ledge instead of taking one thing at a time as he had been taught, Remo slipped. The fourth wall kept moving on, pushing his shoes, and Remo reversed, tumbled and retreated. Retreated past the doors through which he could have broken if he had not been so arrogant.

The truck closed the meager space, driving several garbage cans in front of it. The garbage cans would crumble when the truck met the end wall. Remo would be splattered into the wall. The front steel plate caught part of the uneven alley wall, and chipped brick went flying forward.

Ten feet now, and the truck was coming on. Ten feet to maneuver and there was oil in his shoes from the fall. Six feet, and the steel plate loomed overhead cutting out the sun, making Remo's small room that much darker. Remo kicked off the slippery-soled shoes and moved forward into the metal plate with the painted truck front. Speed forward, the up-jump with the hands high, feel the top of the false front and neatly over to the hood, fast, in one movement like a cat, and there he was staring at two suddenly shocked men in the cab, one of them behind the wheel, both of them very unfortunate.

The truck cracked into the wall with a thud, shivering the surrounding buildings. But Remo was not on the hood. He was in the air above it just an eighth of an inch when the impact came. The drivers, despite bracing themselves, slammed into the windshield of the cab. Remo came back down gently. The drivers lunged for the cab doors, but the narrow alley locked them in.

The man riding shotgun to the driver tried to squeeze out of his window space but his torso got wedged halfway between wall and cab.

'You lose,' said Remo, and the man's head suddenly spurted blood from nose and eyes and mouth, which is normal for someone who has just had his skull crushed between brick wall and a hand as hard as steel and as fast as a bullet.

The driver was stuck, too. He couldn't make it out his window side. His puffy red face contorted in terror. He tried to make it out the other window. But there was a body there.

'You've got an interesting problem there, buddy,' said Remo. He squatted down close to the window. The driver covered his face, waiting for a blow. When he peeked out from behind his arms, there was Remo, still peering at him as if examining a paramecium or a chess move. No hate. No anger. Just interest.

'Arc you going to come out or am I going to have to come in there after you?' asked Remo.

The driver lunged beneath the dashboard and came up with a forty-five, but his target was no longer on the hood. Where the hell was he? Then the driver felt a hand tickle his neck sort of, and then he felt nothing.

Remo scampered over the flat metal roof of the trailer. A head peered out of a window three stories up.

'Driver trainees. They took a wrong turn,' yelled Remo to the person looking down at an alley full of truck. He took the jump in a straight down instead of going forward with the momentum. As soon as he hit the alley entrance he was walking normally and looking back like any other bystander puzzled by the loud noise and an alleywide truck, stuck there like a broad broad in a girdle.

'Traffic is becoming impossible in Chicago,' Remo muttered indignantly. Down the street, he saw the unmistakable waddle of his friend, the Pig, who *would* take a hefty coffin. Pigarello obviously had waited for the crash, then without looking back lest he appear guilty, had walked purposefully away, the only person on the block not looking at the alley. Remo caught up to Pigarello in a few moments. He couldn't lose him. He fell in, step to step, behind the Pig. The Pig got into a four-door sedan furtively, as furtively as a rolling, waddling pumpkin could. Remo opened the back door as the Pig opened the front door. The sounds coincided. The Pig stared straight ahead. So did the driver, whose neck was wet from perspiration. Remo eased down just beneath the line of mirror sight.

'Okay, Siggy. That's it for the kid.'

'Good,' said the driver. He pulled out into the traffic and passed two police cars going in the opposite direction, their sirens ablaze.

'You know,' said the driver. 'I never did this stuff before. Most of us never had anything to do with anything like this before. I don't like it. I just don't like it. I just never thought this thing would go this far. First one, then another, then another, and it never ends. This isn't unionism.'

'You eat good?' asked the Pig.

'Yeah. I eat. But I ate good before.'

'Nobody stuck a gun in your face to make you do these things,' said the Pig. 'You did them. We do them. Companies do them. Loan sharks do them. Numbers bankers do them. Everybody does them.'

'I never did them before, and with rare exceptions, neither do any other locals.'

'So?'

'So, I don't like it.'

'Tough titty,' said the Pig. 'It's life.'

Gene Jethro was waiting in the garage of his hotel when the car with his two men (and the man they were sent to get if they could) pulled in. He gave everyone a big Gene Jethro smile.

'How are you all?' asked Jethro.

'We're okay. It all worked out fine,' said the Pig.

'Good. I hate violence. That's a disruption of the flow of life,' said Jethro. The Pig looked puzzled. He reached to meet Jethro's hand which was coming through the car window. The hand went by him. The hand went to the back seat. Rocco 'the Pig' Pigarello's eyes followed the hand to the back seat. He fainted.

'Oh, gracious Lord,' said the pale-faced driver. Sigmund Negronski, who suddenly noticed that there was someone in the back seat and that someone was the man he had been feeling guilty about killing. 'Gracious Lord,' he said again.

Remo shook Jethro's hand.

'Hmmm,' said Remo. 'You. I thought so.'

'Glad to meetcha, fella,' said Jethro. His love beads dangled over his pale madras blouse.

'Can't stay,' said Remo. 'Gotta run.'

'Hey, baby. I'm welcoming you to the family. Don't

leave so soon.'

'Gotta run,' said Remo.

'I'm offering you a job.'

'Got more important things,' said Remo.

'There's nothing more important than the drivers,' said Jethro. Remo slid from the car and walked out of the garage to the street with Jethro following.

'Hey, wait. Wait,' called Jethro. 'Where are you running to?'

'Got to get a three-stone duck,' said Remo. He accosted a woman. Would she know where there was a poultry store? Supermarket? queried the woman. No, said Remo. Poultry store. The woman pointed. Two blocks, she said. She was pointing east. Remo followed the finger and the new president of the International Brotherhood of Drivers followed Remo.

'Two blocks east,' said Remo. 'The woman said two blocks east.'

'This union has got a future. You've got a future. We're going places and you can go places with us. Now how about it?'

'There it is,' said Remo, pointing to a store which had a horizontal necklace of yellowish, plucked birds strung in the window.

'The truth is that you're known as a stand-up guy, and I'm a bit suspicious of you. I want you on my team or out of the union. Now I'm being honest with you. I want you to be honest with me.'

'A two-and-a-half-pound duck,' Remo said to the proprietor.

'You want the giblets?'

'I don't know. I guess so.'

'Look,' whispered Jethro. 'I'll level further. If you hadn't come with Pigarello and Negronski, you'd be a dead man now. How's that for leveling?'

Remo wiped his ear.

'That looks pretty small for two and a half pounds.'

'That's two and a half pounds,' said the owner wiping

his hands on his entrail-splattered white smock.

'Okay. If you say so,' said Remo.

'Now I tell you. You've gotten to me, dude. I'll make the offer once more for the last time. You're either my recording secretary or a corpse.'

Remo looked at Jethro. He studied the face. He bit his lower lip in deep concentration and study.

'Does that look like two and a half pounds to you?' he asked.

'Jeeezuz,' wailed Gene Jethro. 'What is the matter with you? You have got to be the loosest dude I have ever unshaded my orbs for.'

'Does that mean you think it looks like two and a half pounds?'

Jethro sighed. 'Okay. I'll look.' He stood on his toes to peer over the counter at the yellowish fowl being encased in thick white paper.

'Yeah, two and a half pounds,' he said. 'Now. Death or the job.'

'You only gave it a little peek,' said Remo. 'I mean one look, and you say yes. How can I trust you? What do you know about fowl? What do you know about ducks? What do you know about anything?'

'All right,' said Jethro. 'It's your life.' He shrugged and walked to the door.

'Hey, sweetheart, the truck with the funny steel front doesn't work.'

Jethro stopped as though slapped by a wet pontoon. He stared at Remo, openmouthed.

'That funny truck with the unfunny alley. It doesn't work. I only went along with Pigarello to see who sent him. Although I really knew.' Remo took the package from the owner, and felt the heft of the duck.

'Light,' he said. He struck the bird under his arm and strolled out the door, past a shocked Gene Jethro.

By the time Remo was scampering through traffic, Jethro had caught up with him. The usually calm and cool face was now a red mask of rage.

'All right, you sonuvabitch. What's your price?'

'I'll think about it, okay?'

'Well. You better do some real fancy thinking if you want to see your gook nutritionist again. Yeah. I know about him. I sent some of my people over to him to explain why he should come with us. Now if you need him for a special diet, buddy, and I figure it's got to be very special and very necessary otherwise you wouldn't bring him with you, if you really need him, you better start naming some prices for your services.'

'How many men did you send?'

'Three. One to carry him, one to look out, and one to drive.'

'Hmmm,' said Remo. He asked a passerby for a luggage store.

'Just four stores over,' he was told. He went, Jethro followed.

'Yes, sir. Can I help you?' asked the clerk.

'Yeah,' said Remo. He turned to Jethro. 'How big were the men?'

'Why do you ask. Ah, forget it. One 5′ 10″, one 6′ 1″, and one 6′ 6″,'

Remo ordered three trunks, one very long.

Chiun wanted to be a writer. He pondered upon the possibility of this career during a commercial. He would tell the world of a man who wished to be alone with beauty. A man whom the moons of time had made desirous of only the gentlest beauty. A man who asked little for himself and gave much. A man who saw in a wild and boisterous land a glorious art form which thrilled the soul. This poor old wise and beloved man wanted nothing more than to be allowed the few precious moments of peace in which to spend his declining years appreciating the beautiful stories of 'Edge of Dawn,' 'As the Planet Revolves,' and 'Dr. Lawrence Walters, Psychiatrist.'

Then upon this wonderfully sweet and most gentle man did thoughtlessly burst in three crude and cruel villains. They cared not for the beauty of drama. They cared not for the few meager pleasures of this sweet, wise, beloved old man. They cared only for their villainous, cruel and despicable schemes. They stole light from the box which gave the art. With disdain, they pressed the button which made beauty no more. With cruel heartlessness they stole the beloved wise man's only little joy.

So what could this beloved creature do, but arrange as best he could to watch the show in peace?

Ah, but the story was not finished. Would an ungrateful, lazy student understand this? Would he care that the Master of Sinanju, who had given him knowledge beyond that of any white man, lost the one true meager pleasure of his sparse life? No. He would not. He would concern himself with who picked up this piece of something. Or who picked up that piece of something. Or who did which cleaning chore or the other. That is what the ingrate would concern himself with. That was his nature. That was his character.

Ah, if only Chiun could tell this story to the world in word pictures. Then, others might understand the plight of a sweet, beloved old man.

The door to the hotel suite opened. The Master of Sinanju would not lower himself to petty haggling. The door slammed shut.

'Chiun. If I've told you once, I've told you a thousand times. If you kill 'em, you clean 'em up,' said Remo.

The Master of Sinanju refused to be drawn into the haggling.

'What with the Supreme Court decision, there's now only one crime in America punishable by death. Turning off your sloshy little soap operas.'

The Master of Sinanju would not be provoked to name-calling.

'Will you answer me? Did you do a job on these guys because they turned off your soap opera?'

The Master of Sinanju refused to indulge in recriminations.

'Chiun. This has got to stop. I mean it.'

The Master of Sinanju would overlook the disrespect shown.

'Will you help me get them into these trunks?'

The Master of Sinanju refused to do cleaning chores of a woman after being thoroughly insulted.

'Sometimes, Chiun, I hate you.'

The Master of Sinanju had known this all along, otherwise why should the ungrateful pupil care so little for the few meager pleasures of an old man. Ah, to be a writer.

TEN

At 12.12 P.M. in Chicago that day, two men reported upstairs. Remo open-coded Smith over the telephone, informed him that he saw an alternate to the extreme plan and would like to proceed.

'I think I can get to the core of the apple and manipulate the seeds without having to make the whole thing into apple sauce,' said Remo.

'Go ahead,' said Smith.

Gene Jethro had received the report from Pigarello and Negronski.

'I didn't even hear him get in the car, and I was driving,' said Negronski.

'Two good men were in the cab of that truck,' said the Pig. 'Good stand-up guys. They knew what they were doing, too. They lowered the plate real good. I had some guys check later. Everything from bottles to garbage cans was mashed in that alley. Except the kid, that Remo Jones.'

'So what are you telling me?'

'I'm telling you I don't want to go against that guy again.'

'Same here,' said Negronski.

Jethro played with his love beads. He had lost three men on the nutritionist, too. It was weird. It approached powers he could not handle. He thanked Pigarello and Negronski, saying he would get back to them later. He made a fast dash by car to the new building. He said the proper words and was let in. He took the elevator to the main basement floor by pressing the combination of numbers.

The sign under the map was illuminated with spots from the ceiling. If the far wall were slid open, as it could be when the last electrical wiring was fixed, it would open to a meeting room just smaller than convention hall.

Jethro did not see the need for such a secure hall at such an expense, but thoroughness was thoroughness. Now was not the time to alter plans.

His footsteps clicked on the new linoleum as he walked past the special room, hardly giving it a glance. Just before the sliding wall was a door. Jethro knocked three times. Nothing. He knocked again. Nothing.

He opened the door and entered a small oasis of greenery, of pleasantly tinkling air chimes, of cool incense wafting to his senses. A waterfall over carefully placed rocks gurgled into a pool. He shut the door behind him and searched the indoor garden. Nothing. Artificial sunlight without heat illuminated the room with a bluish cast. Jethro blinked his eyes.

'You have eyes, but cannot see,' came a voice.

Jethro peered into heavy shrubbery near the waterfall.

'Ears, but cannot hear.'

Jethro tried to follow the voice.

'Over here by the pool.'

Jethro looked again, surprised that he had not seen him the first time. He sat, his legs crossed, on a large rock. A book was in his lap. He wore a conservative gray suit, with white shirt and striped tie. Jethro should have spotted him immediately. The face was flat and smooth and Oriental.

'Uh, I came to tell you we can't go at that guy Remo again. We'll just have to live with him.'

'Did he accept your offer?'

'No.'

'Then why do you come here?'

'To tell you.'

'You were supposed to enlist him or eliminate him. You have not been able to enlist him, so really you have only one other course of action.'

'We failed.'

'Then try again. What success was ever achieved without a failure? I tell you success comes from learning what will not work. If every man surrendered to the happenstance of fate, we would all be living in caves because the first house fell down.'

'I'm afraid of this man.'

'Good. It shows you have a mind.'

'I do not wish to send men against him again.'

'You mean you find it unpleasant.'

'Yes.'

'So is birth and so even are the better forms of love at some point in love-making. I tell you there is nothing of worth that does not try your soul. Go ahead and do this thing. Earn the power you will receive.'

'Yes, Nuihc,' said Jethro, but while the words made sense they did not convince his heart. 'Yes, Nuihc. I will do as you say, as always.'

Sigmund Negronski morosely played with his iced sherbet as Jethro told the assembled wives of the driver leadership that 'behind the man who is behind the man who drives the truck is the woman.'

'A union wife is one of the most important assets an officer of a local can have. She is the one to whom we look to make the International Brotherhood of Drivers the most successful union in the history of the labor movement. I thank you.'

Applause, at first polite then growing, then resounding.

Gene Jethro, draped in beige polka dots, blew the women kisses. They blew kisses back.

He sat down near Negronski on the speaker's dais, still smiling at the driver wives.

'Pretty good, huh, Siggy?' he said, still smiling and blowing specific kisses to specific wives. His own girl friend had worn a modest sheath, the consistency of cheesecloth, and she was braless. She smiled silently at his side.

'I'm worried. What do we need this Remo guy for? Those guys they pulled from the horse of the tractor trailer had their heads crushed.'

'I know. I know. I don't want him, either.'

'Then let's forget about him.'

'We can't.'

'We gonna go at him again?'

'We'll have to.'

'But why? He seems as though he is willing to be left alone. He doesn't bother you unless you bother him.'

'I know. You're right. I think you're 100 percent absolutely correct. I'd like to ignore him also.'

'Then why don't we.'

'Because we can't. We got to do what we got to do. And don't think I'm not a wee bit scared now, also.'

Jethro rose again and, blowing kisses, yelled:

'Love ya. Love ya all.'

A waiter made his way behind the speaker's dais. He carried no tray. His hands were at his sides. He slipped Gene Jethro a crumpled piece of paper.

'Telephone message, sir.'

Jethro took it, and the artificial smile became suddenly warm and real.

'Siggy. We don't have to go at him again,' Jethro said. 'He says he wants to join.'

Dr. Harold Smith threw up his lunch and part of what he believed was his breakfast. He staggered back from the sink in his Folcroft office to the television set, then pressed for a rerun of the news show. That done, he pressed for a rerun of the three major network news shows. Then he ran back to his office bathroom. He flooded his mouth with a strong disinfectant and played the Thursday evening news shows again, just to make sure he had not gone insane and was hallucinating.

Unfortunately, he was sane. There, flickering on the screen, the man who was executed so that he would not exist, the man who was under orders to kill immediately anyone who might recognize him despite the face operations, the killer arm of the organization to whom public knowledge meant total defeat of itself and a way of government, was standing before microphones, yelling into microphones, the center of attention of an entire convention. The new recording secretary. The new look in the drivers' union. One of the new young mods, according to one announcer, Remo Jones. And Remo Jones was saying a mouthful.

Remo Jones felt that old unionism was dead.

'The day of the muscleman and the bought contract is over,' said Remo. 'The day when the driver was considered the big dumb servant of an industry is over. The day this nation took for granted the services of so many loyal workers is over. There is a new driver and he is a professional. There is a new union member and he will not settle for the crumbs of the industrial table any more than his father settled for the whips and the guns of the corporate goons.

'I say to you, fellow drivers, fellow officials, and fellow Americans, that we have attained a new consciousness in Gene Jethro, one born of struggle, nurtured in wisdom and harvested in faith, faith that we drivers are only part of a gigantic transportation complex that must work together or die separately. Ask not what your union can do for you, but what you can do for your union.'

The convention rose as one man to hysterically applaud the new recording secretary. Gene Jethro hugged him. Remo hugged Jethro. They hugged each other. They faced the cameras left. They faced the cameras right. They faced the cameras center, their outside arms raised to the ceiling of convention hall.

Those little lights flashing were cameras. Those many little lights flashing were cameras taking Remo's picture for distribution over the world.

Smith groaned. This was to have been the solution. This was to have been the plan to avoid committing the extreme plan. Remo was to penetrate the high command of the drivers and stop the formation of the monster union from within the key union, the International Brotherhood of Drivers. Remo was to take a post, not parade in it.

At the time, it seemed like a better solution than the murder of four union officials. Smith had allowed it. Encouraged it. But what he had not encouraged was this sudden streak of exhibitionism. Smith flicked on one of the still shots. There was the secret human superweapon happier than Smith had ever seen him, like a publicity junkie on a fix. The man who had been publicly executed so that he would not exist!

Smith should have suspected this possibility. A man who did not exist, who could not even keep one face for more than a year. Give him a little public recognition and he would be delirious with new-found joy. Hadn't he complained about the face changes, longing to return to his original appearance? That was a sign. The hostile expression of his humanity. That was a sign. And now this.

Dr. Harold Smith looked at the beaming face, and for a moment felt a winsome pang of warmth for Remo, a very small and very distant wish that this man who had served the organization so well, could some day indulge himself in his human desires.

This pang was very fleeting, however. Remo was going to get them killed. Exposure meant death. That had been built into the organization. There would be no living witnesses but the President.

Dr. Smith gazed at the face, the exuberant joy, the

open, delicious enjoyment of fame, and Dr. Smith turned away from the set.

Then he remembered to turn off the set, and made a pencil note to himself that the set should be rigged to turn itself off automatically. After all, imagine if someone were to enter this office and see that face frozen on the screen. Why Remo wasn't even allowed ever to return to Folcroft.

The very thought of all the precautions taken depressed him.

The special line rang.

'Yes sir,' said Dr. Smith.

'It seems as if nothing has happened to delay what I feared,' came the voice famous to millions of Americans, the voice they heard in State of the Union messages, on national addresses, the voice that told them their nation had a leader.

'It will not come to pass, sir.'

'I would have hoped that it would have been stopped by now.'

'Anything else, sir.'

'No. That's all.'

'If it will make you feel any better, sir, we will have the danger removed before the planned announcement tomorrow.'

'Then they are going to create that union, aren't they?'

'Sir, good-bye.'

Dr. Smith hung up. He checked his watch. Two more minutes. He flicked on the computer readout. The first paragraphs dealt with a stock swindle by a major corporation. In all his years as director of the organization, he privately estimated that big business stole more than seventeen times the amount that outside organized crime did. But business was easier to handle. A leak to a newspaper columnist would stop the richest and most powerful business in the country. A set of engineering plans for a faulty car that one corporate giant had failed to recall, hoping the flaw would not be exposed, lest the callback cut into profits. That one had been fun. It was addressed to a famous muckraking columnist but delivered to the desk of the motor company president. He scarcely had the envelope open before he ordered the callback.

In the sight of the organization, a faulty car was mass murder.

The telephone rang.

'Hello there, fella,' came Remo's voice, brimming with new joy. 'Did you catch the evening news?'

'I did,' said Smith dryly.

'I have to say it. I was fantastic. I had them eating out of my hands. What did you think of the speech?'

'Routine,' said Smith.

'Routine, hell. A standing ovation of seven minutes. The head of the American Legion only got three minutes and Jethro himself barely got eight minutes on his inauguration speech yesterday. You see the way Jethro hugged me on the podium. He had to. Couldn't let me walk away with the convention.'

'If I may interrupt your political career for a moment, how do we stand on the survival of the nation?'

'Oh, that. Don't sweat. Will do. They have yet to present a problem which our resources cannot overcome. They have yet to build the barricade we cannot storm, the wall we cannot scale, the weapon we cannot smash. We are a new generation, born in...'

'You have until tomorrow,' said Dr. Harold Smith and slammed down the phone. Remo had gone from assassin to politician without ever stopping at human.

Remo heard the click of the phone. He hung up the receiver and looked at Chiun. Chiun had thought his song was beautiful, confessed that when he was young in Sinanju he had daydreamed of becoming a great political leader. Chiun rose and mounted a hotel bed. His arms waved and he began an oration, the rough translation being, 'Drive the villainous oppressors from sacred Korea.'

'That's pretty good,' said Remo. 'Did you give it often?'

'I gave it not at all. You see we assassins of Sinanju usually worked for the oppressors. My father heard me once in a field, practicing, and he explained that the oppressor put food on our table. The oppressor put a roof over our head. Without discord and violence, the entire economy of Sinanju would be bankrupt. In many ways, Sinanju is a little corner of the rest of the world.'

'The greatest assassins who have ever lived, Master of Sinanju,' said Remo.

Chiun bowed politely, accepting the accolade which was naturally due from anyone wise enough to perceive such a truth.

'I got work tonight. I'll be out. You want me to bring back something?'

'Bring back victory in your teeth,' said Chiun, and Remo laughed. They would sometimes watch movies on television and the violent ones were the funniest. One of the lines in a war movie was, 'Bring back victory in your teeth.' It was so amateurish, Chiun never forgot it.

'I'll bring back some wild rice, perhaps. And maybe some cod.'

'Cod is oily,' said Chiun. 'Try and do some work with the elbows tonight.'

'Why, am I losing something?'

'No. It's just good to work the elbows from time to time. Try haddock. Don't forget. We had halibut Monday.'

'Yes, little father.'

And Remo left Chiun orating to himself on the bed, about the poor man throwing off the shackles of the oppressor until all men walked in peace and freedom and beauty.

The building was not hard to find. It was surrounded by an electric fence twelve feet high, lit by yellow floods in a muggy gray night, smelling of fresh-turned sod and new-planted trees. Remo set the double-wrapped bag of fish behind a small bush, and upjumped, right hand high, to one of the pole tips supporting the fence. He balanced on the tip, his right arm straight beneath him, his legs outstretched to avoid the electric current. It was the nature of electric fences that the supporting poles were insulators, thus making the fences effective barriers against only those people who did not normally practice getting through them. An electric fence, thought Remo, was a filter to keep out the harmless.

He surveyed the bottom ground with a practiced eye. No planted little device on the other side, but to be sure, he single hand jumped a good twelve feet out and landed like a cat, quick, smooth and moving. Over a little knoll he saw the building. It rose, metal glinting into the moonlight like four vertical aluminum coffins with brass trimming. Its base was floodlit.

Remo moved over the new, fresh earth, with the smooth silence of many years of practice, hardly thinking, letting his body do what it knew how to do. He crossed the cement driveway with the feet themselves looking for the pebbles that could cause the attention-getting scrape, then on to the base of the building, behind the floodlight, where he stood in darkness. Ten stories it was, and the windows without grips or ledges but set flush into the wall like a smooth carpenter's-joint.

Not bad. Remo sidemoved to the corner, scampering over a hose left carelessly for the morning dew. The air reeked of fresh paint and acids used to polish the building wall.

If he couldn't get in from the bottom, then he would enter from the top. No one defended an isolated building from a top entrance. He wrapped himself around the corner, placing the ridges of his open palms against the cool metal and pressing his knees directly into, not downward but into, the metal walls. While the hands uplifted the knees maintained.

Simultaneously his body moved, one simple complete

jerk of all the appropriate muscles, then another. In and out, in and out, he began to rise like a jigsaw going through wood. Rapidly to the point where extra energy decreased upward speed and then more slowly for the maximum rise, keeping the rhythm perfect and the momentum going up, press in, release, in, release, in, release, hands bringing up, legs holding, the smell of the wall against his cheek, the cool metal going down along his stomach, the top of the building coming closer and then, the edge of the gutter, grab up, and over, feet up, and leaning against the gutter, and looking down at the floods ten stories below him.

Let's hear it for me, he said, wishing Chiun had been there. Of course, Chiun would never admit the quality of the rise. But just his negation of it would be a compliment. Remo brushed off his hands. The palms were slightly burned. Damn. He certainly didn't want to have to go down with burned palms. The descent was far more difficult.

Remo swung down from the gutter and felt the top of the topmost window with his feet. Smooth. No ledge. No opening. Impossible. He worked his way along the gutter, a spider-gliding man ten stories high, his feet feeling for window ledges, openings, something. At the corners of the building, he kicked around and still no openings. The four sides, ten stories high, were like the front, defended. He would have to kick in.

He selected the center of the closest window and tapped it for sound. The glass sounded soft, no sharp hard response to the sole of his shoe. He was afraid of that. It might be glass. It might not be glass. He did not want to come into a window and bounce back ten stories high. Too chancy.

There were old assassins and bold assassins, as Chiun had said. But there were no old bold assassins. It was the mark of amateurism to risk one's life unnecessarily. Remo pulled his body up to the roof. He felt along the sloping metal. Nothing. He shimmied to the apex. Nothing.

He would have to descend with damaged palms, the key instrument in wall movement. Or he could wait, he thought, until next day someone said:

'What is that idiot doing on that roof ten stories high and how did he get there?'

Remo blew on his palms and swung down over the gutter. *Here we go,* he thought, and taking extra precaution, pushed too hard and felt himself go away from the building and free-fall momentarily until he glided his body back to the metal edge. He would have to friction cut the fall until he got a grip or landed. The way to get killed was to try to stop the fall completely, as a normal person might.

About the third story, he lost the friction cut completely and had to take the fall with a decompression of the legs. He landed in the soft earth, but with a stinging, sharp pain in his ribs and chest. The feet were buried to the ankles. Remo eased himself out, limping.

He would have to risk a door where he could be seen. He tried the door. It was locked, naturally, but when he tried to smash his way through, he discovered that the doors were not metal but a yielding latticework that surrendered to his hands, then repelled them. He tried the windows from the ground. Lucky he had not tried them fully from the roof. No entrance.

At the fence, a guard was waiting by Remo's package of fish.

'Enjoying yourself?' asked the guard.

'What are you doing with my haddock?'

'What are you doing on restricted grounds?'

'Looking for my haddock,' said Remo, snatching the bag from a guard who could have sworn he had a secure grip on it.

'I'm going to have to take you in.'

'Do not bother me,' said Remo. 'I am frustrated at this moment and I do not wish to be bothered. I must confess failure to the one person in the world to whom I hate to confess failure.'

'You got other problems, sonny. Breaking and entering, trespassing and if I say so, assault upon my person.'

'What?' said Remo, trying to formulate an explanation for Chiun.

'Assault upon my person,' said the guard.

'Okay,' said Remo. He broke the guard's face and trotted back into the city.

Chiun smiled at first when he heard of Remo's failure. He laid this to early, impure eating habits, to disrespect for the master, to failure to understand the beauty of the great American art form. But as Remo went over detail by detail his approach to entering the building and as Chiun nodded that each step was correct, a deep grimness appeared on the old man's face.

'So what did I do wrong?' asked Remo.

Chiun was silent a moment. Then very slowly he spoke.

'My son. It is with heavy heart, great sadness, and shame for the Master of Sinanju that I must tell you, you have done nothing wrong. You have done right, and the wisdom given you was inadequate for the task. The disgrace is upon me and my family.'

'But it's just a building. You had me practice on atomic installations.'

'Those installations were designed to prohibit the entrance of people who used guns and cars and tanks and various implements of Western technology. This building was designed to repel us.'

'But who the hell in this country knows the methods of Sinanju?'

'Some know Ninji,' said Chiun, referring to the Japanese art that teaches people to move at night and penetrate castles.

'But the teaching of Ninji is only part of Sinanju.'

Chiun was silent. 'I myself must look.'

'That's all we need from the building for now. I'll work it from the other end, from Jethro,' said Remo. 'And, little father . . .'

'Yes?' said the Master of Sinanju preparing to darken his face and don the robes of the dark so that he could become part of the night.

'Bring home victory in your teeth,' said Remo.

ELEVEN

The hardware stores were closed. Remo had to open one. He went through the front door of a little shop around the corner from his hotel, because it had a special kind of burglar alarm that held a special kind of guarantee for Remo. If the door were snapped open very quickly and then closed again just as quickly, the alarm turned itself off and one could walk right in.

Remo selected a Stanley crowbar about three feet long, $4.98. He forgot whether there was a sales tax in Chicago or how much that tax would be, so he left $5, assuming that he had saved the owner a salesman's fee. He wrapped the crowbar in brown paper, careful not to touch it with his bare hands. Then he slipped from the shop, resetting the alarm, and went to Abe Bludner's room.

Bludner had a suite in the same hotel as Remo and Chiun.

Remo knocked on Bludner's door.

'Who is it?' came Stanziani's voice.

'Remo.'

'What do you want?'

'I want to see Bludner.'

'He's not in.'

'Open the door.'

'I said he's not in.'

'Either you'll open the door, or I'll open the door, but the door is going to open.'

'You want a table in your face?'

'If you have to open the door to throw it, yes.'

The door opened and a heavy, lacquered coffee table came flying through it. Remo caught the table's center with his free left hand. A little chop down its center. Split.

Stanziani stood in the doorway in gray slacks and sports shirt. He looked at the left side of the table against the far wall, and the right side near the door. Then he looked at Remo and smiled weakly. A dark stain began to spread in the crotch of his grey slacks.

'Hi,' he said.

'Hi,' said Remo.

'Wanna come in?' asked Tony.

'Yeah,' said Remo. 'I thought you'd never ask.'

A voice bellowed from another room.

'Did you let in the kid? I told you I didn't want to let in the kid.' It was Bludner.

Remo followed the voice to the bedroom. Bludner was part of a three-handed card game. The door to another living room was open. Three middle-aged, matronly women, obviously the wives, were playing cards.

'You must be Remo,' called out one of them. 'I'm Mrs. Bludner. Did you eat? Why didn't Abe tell me you were so cute. Hey, Abe, he's cute. He's the first cute official you've ever had. The rest look like gangsters. Answer me, Abe.'

Bludner shot Remo a baleful look.

'What is it, Dawn?'

'Why didn't you tell me he was so cute? I don't think he's faggy at all. Some weight you could use, however. Did you eat?'

'I ate. Thank you, ma'am. Abe, why didn't you tell me your wife was so attractive.'

Giggles from the living room.

'What do you want, kid?'

'I want to talk to you.'

'I don't want to talk to you.' said Bludner.

'What's wrong?'

'What's this, you come in the driver's union because I

say so and then you're national recording secretary without I even know? What's this?'

'Abe, you know I'm loyal to the local,' said Remo, the politician.

'Loyal to the local, you don't even know the local.'

'Abe, you should be happy. Now the local's got a national officer.'

'I should have been asked. Jethro should have cleared it with me. How does that make me look to my own men, Jethro appointing someone from my local without it being cleared by me.'

'Jethro is a sonuvabitch and I don't trust him,' said Remo, the politician. 'But you can trust me. I'm your man in there,' said Remo the politician.

'Trust you, kid? I don't even know you.'

'Are your feelings hurt?' asked Remo.

'Hurt? How the hell could two young punks like you and Jethro hurt me? I've spit better men than you two out of my mouth. Hey, Tony. Am I hurt?'

'No, boss,' answered Stanziani. He was in the other room, changing.

'Hey, Paul. Am I hurt?'

'No boss,' came a voice from a far off bathroom.

'He's hurt,' came a woman's voice from the living room. Abe Bludner left the cards and shut the door to the living room.

'You really know how to hurt, kid,' said Abe 'Crowbar' Bludner.

'I'm sorry,' said Remo.

'That for me?' asked Bludner.

'This. No. It's for me. It's a crowbar. I'm going to hang it in my office to remind me forever that I owe my career to Abe "Crowbar" Bludner.'

'I don't know whether that's such a good idea,' said Bludner. He reached for the crowbar, and Remo slipped off the paper. Bludner grabbed it and took a few practice swings, like a batter warming up. Then he brought the crowbar a hair from Remo's head with a great swishing of air.

'Scare you, kid?' asked Bludner.

'No,' said Remo. 'I knew you wouldn't hit me, Abe. We're from the same local.'

'Don't you ever forget it, kid. You hear?'

Bludner returned the crowbar and Remo carefully wrapped it without getting his own fingerprints on it. They shook hands and Remo departed. No, Remo did not care to make a pinochle foursome.

He hid the crowbar under the mattress of his hotel bed, careful not to smudge the prints any more than he had to. The crowbar would be for the extreme plan, if all else didn't work.

Jethro now had a whole floor in the posh Delstoyne Hotel across town. The elevators did not stop there unless permission was granted by telephone from the top floor where Jethro was staying. The stairwells were locked. When the recording secretary, Remo Jones, asked permission to see Jethro, this was surprisingly denied because Jethro wasn't in.

'Where is he?' asked Remo.

'He's out.'

'That tells me where he isn't, not where he is. Where is he?'

'I can't say any more. Do you want to leave a message? Where you can be reached?'

'No. I'm coming up.'

'You can't do that, sir. The elevator won't stop and the stairwells are locked.'

'See you in a minute.'

Actually it was closer to five minutes. Remo took his time walking up the steps. The stairwell lock to the eighteenth floor was reinforced by a freshly installed, super-strength padlock.

Remo took the bolts out of the hinges and opened the door from the other side. He handed the startled guard the bolts.

'I'll only be a few minutes,' he said.

'You can't do that. That's breaking and entering.'

'They wouldn't have a name for it if it couldn't be done,' said Remo. The guard tried to grab Remo's shoulder, but the shoulder wasn't there. He tried to grab the shirt collar but that was suddenly just out of reach. He tried to crack the head with a rosewood billy club. Suddenly he felt a sharp pain in his chest, a heavy sinking to the floor, and then he felt nothing.

Remo surveyed the hallway. Jethro was probably in the end room. The reasoning behind this deduction impressed Remo himself. Jethro was the most important man in the driver's union. He would, therefore, have the biggest suite. The biggest suites would have windows looking out on two streets instead of one. Therefore, the Jethro suite would be at the end of the corridor. Remo cracked open the locked door at the end of the corridor.

'Oh, I'm sorry,' he said, staring at a middle-aged man with tousled jet-black hair on his head and graying hair on his crotch. The middle-aged man was on his back and mounted by a svelte young redhead.

'Hi. What can we do for you?' she asked.

'Nothing. I'm looking for Gene Jethro.'

'Where's Jethro?' the redheaded girl asked of her mount.

'You get out of here or I'll call the guard,' yelled the middle-aged man.

'You're position's wrong,' said Remo.

'Bye, sweetie,' said the girl.

Remo shut the door. If Jethro were not at the end, then it stood to reason he would be in the middle.

There were five doors in the hallway. Remo opened the third from the end.

'Oh, sorry,' he said to the tangle of arms and legs that he judged to be four people, three women and a man. He stepped into the room to examine the man's face. Moving aside a rather pendulous breast, he saw the hard-lined face of a man who was not Gene Jethro. The man had the happy grin of a cocaine high. Remo returned the breast and left the room.

He tried another door. Another orgy. Three rooms, three orgies. One room would have been whoopie. Two rooms, an epidemic of whoopie. But for three rooms, there was a plan behind this. It was simple numbers. And if Remo knew who the men were, he would know why the activity. They were obviously supplied women. Three random men just don't happen to orgy score at the same time. The women were probably assigned to keep them in their rooms.

Remo looked down the hallway. The crumpled figure of the guard began to stir. They were probably the other union chiefs, kept nice and safe and occupied here in Jethro's suite until tomorrow's announcement of the superunion. And if Remo did not succeed, they would all become gristle and cracked bone between a fallen beam and platform.

The guard staggered to his feet.

'What hit me?'

Remo trotted to him, grabbing him by the collar. He pressured nerves in the neck until the guard emitted a little helpless groan.

'Where's Jethro's apartment?' Remo asked.

'Second from the end.'

'Why that one?'

'It's the biggest suite,' said the guard.

'Oh,' said Remo and put the guard to sleep again.

Jethro's suite was indeed the largest. The plushly carpeted living room, draperies at the windows and paintings on the wall, contained the kind of furniture that could wreck a bank account.

'Is that you, honey?' It was a woman's voice, muffled by a door.

'Yes,' said Remo, since he felt very much like a honey

at the time.

'I've got soap in my eyes. Will you hand me a towel?'

Of course, Remo would hand her a towel. He wasn't a sadist.

He opened the door whence the voice came and immediately was hit by steam. The mirrors were fogged. The tile walls dripped, and a shower ran full and hot. A delicate hand poked from behind the shower curtain. Remo put a towel in it.

'How did it go today, dear?'

'Okay.'

'It looks as if it's all going to work out, doesn't it? I mean you won't have any more trouble from that rotten, awful man.'

'No,' said Remo.

'What does he want from you anyway? You've done everything you're supposed to.'

Remo cocked an ear.

'What?' he said.

'What does he want from you anyway?'

'Who?'

'Who do you think I'm talking about? Mick Jagger? You know, Nuihc.'

So there was someone else. So maybe it wasn't this driver leader who designed the building? So why would Remo ever think that a Western man born into Western technology would ever be able to construct a building defended against a force he knew nothing about?

'Did he phone?' Remo would get his whereabouts if he could.

The hand crumpled the shower curtain. A wet, blond head peeked out. It was a beautiful head, with smooth cheeks and blue eyes and voluptuous lips now turned into a smile. The left breast was well formed, too. Firm and rising with symmetrical, light-pink nipple.

'You're not Gene,' said the woman. The smile went.

'I see you got the soap out of your eyes.'

'Get out of here. Get out of here now.'

'I don't want to,' said Remo.

'Get out of here or I'll call the guard.'

'Go ahead.'

'Guard. Guard. Guard,' shrieked the woman.

'My name's Remo, what's yours?'

'You won't be around here long enough to find out. Guard. Guard.'

'Until he comes, tell me your name.'

The beautiful young face was anger and frustration. No guard was coming.

'Will you get out of here? Will you please get out of here?' Now she put on her stern face. It was also beautiful.

'Look. I don't know what sort of kicks you get from watching women bathe, but would you please get out of here?'

Now the supplicating, pained face. Still beautiful.

'All right. What do you want?'

Now the businesswoman.

'Who's Nuihc?'

'I can't tell you. Would you go please?'

Remo shook his head.

'Aw c'mon, mister. If Gene comes back and finds you here, he'll kill you.'

'Maybe he'll tell me who Nuihc is.'

'You wanna find out who Nuihc is, there's a building just outside the city. He's there.'

'I've been there.'

'Bullshit, you've been there. I know you haven't been there, wise guy. Now get out of here before Gene comes back.'

'What's your name?'

'Chris. Now get out of here. At least, let me get dressed.'

'Okay, you can get dressed. I'll be outside.'

'Gee, you're generous,' said Chris.

Remo stole a kiss on her wet cheek, ducking a roundhouse left. He waited in the living room, and waited in the living room, and waited in the living room.

'Are you coming out?'

'Just a second. Just a second,' said Chris.

The door opened and Chris, her blond hair flowing like gracious silk, her body sheathed in white transparent filament, floated into the room. Exquisite.

'I can see more of you dressed than in the shower.'

'Drives you up a wall, doesn't it?' said Chris triumphantly.

Remo cocked his head. He thought a moment.

'Yes,' he said. 'Be nice and I'll make love to you.'

'Don't you wish you could?'

'I can.'

'Don't you wish I'd help you?'

'You will.'

'You're pretty sure of yourself.'

'It's part of the biz, sweetheart.'

'Want a drink?'

'I'm on a diet.'

'I'd offer you something to eat but nobody can go in or out without Gene's okay.'

'We can.'

'No. The whole place is sealed. Until tomorrow at noon, when everyone's going over to that building that you say you've been to.'

Remo nodded. 'What's you favorite food.'

'Are you kidding? Italian.'

'I know a great Italian restaurant in Cicero.'

'We can't get out of here.'

'Lasagna, dripping with cheese and red sauce.'

'I don't like lasagna. I like spaghetti in clam sauce and lobster fra diavola and veal marsala.'

'I know a place where the clams swim in garlic butter and the veal melts wine-tasty in your mouth,' said Remo.

'Let's kill the guard,' said Chris laughing.

'Put some clothes on over your clothes.'

'I was only joking,' said Chris.

'And the lobster swims in a bath of red sauce.'

'I'll wear a coat,' said Chris.

When they passed the guard in the hallway, Chris put a delicate hand to her soft lips.

'I didn't mean that about the guard.'

'I know,' said Remo. 'He just went to sleep for a little while.'

They tiptoed laughing down the steps like youngsters playing hookie. Remo 'borrowed' a car in the hotel garage by jumping the wires.

'You're awful,' laughed Chris. 'When Gene finds out, are you gonna get it. Am I gonna get it.'

'The bread crackles when you break it to soak up the sauce,' said Remo.

'I know a shortcut to Cicero,' said Chris. 'I was born there.'

They talked as they drove, Remo checking his watch. Chris loved Gene, loved him more than any man in her life. She had known many. But there was something just, you know, nice about Gene. Like Remo was nice in a way but too much of a wise guy. Could Remo understand that? Remo could. She had fallen in love with Jethro before he started to change, and when he did start to change about two months ago, she loved him anyway. She couldn't stop loving him. She wanted to stop loving him after the...

'Yes.'

'Never mind. It's something I don't want to say.'

'Okay,' said Remo. They drove in silence until Chris continued.

'You know I never used to wear clothes like this. Gene started liking them about two months ago when he started doing those funny things like breathing exercises and all sorts of nonsense.'

'Does he scream when he lets out the air?' asked Remo.

'Yeah. How do you know?'

'I know,' said Remo. 'I know too well. All too well.'

'Well, I don't like wearing these clothes,' said Chris, unaware of Remo's remark. She was too much in herself. 'I like to keep myself for Gene. But he likes to show off too much. Like I'm another piece of jewelry. I don't like that.'

'Then dress the way you want.'

'He said I'd dress the way he wants or he'd walk.'

'Then you don't need him.'

'Oh, I need him. I need him more than any man in my life. Especially now. You don't know the way he makes love. No man makes love like him. It's more than beautiful; it's so great, it's horrible.'

They found the restaurant, and Remo had water while Chris went through second helpings of linguini. On the way back, Remo parked beside the road. Before she could say no, he slid a smooth hand across her stomach, then covered her lips with his. Working his hand to her thighs and his mouth to her breast, he brought her to slow, inexorable passion, brought her, undressed, to demanding him, begging for him, screaming for him, groaning for him, until he was inside her, her passionate body throbbing with exquisite, unbearable desire for fulfillment.

'Ohhh. Ohhh.' She groaned and her head pressed into the car door, her writhing body making wet marks on the vinyl seat. 'Ahh. Ahhh.' Her fingernails bit into his back and neck, her eyes closing and opening, her mouth open for groaning and air, and biting. She kicked the steering wheel and banged her fists against his head, and cried and yelled, and slammed her hips upward begging for more and more. And when she reached her heights, Remo with two quick, masterful strokes brought her to sobbing, shrieking conclusion.

'Oh. Oh. Oh. More. Give me more. I'm here.'

She softened to limpness and was kissing his ear when Remo ran his tongue down her neck, across her shoulder and down to the hardened nipple. His right hand caressed her hip and then imperceptibly he began to build tension in her again, and fire it, and build it, until she was banging her own head against the door guard, begging for more and faster. Then Remo moved faster, with speed and friction rare for the untrained, but creating a wild heat within her so that she suddenly became stiff and rigid and could not move, just stayed stretched like a bolted board, until her face suddenly contorted, her mouth opened, and there was no scream. Just a sinking down into the car seat where she cried with delirious happiness. It was a good few moments before she spoke and when she did, she was hoarse.

'Remo. Oh, Remo. Oh, Remo. No one was ever like that. You're beautiful.'

He caressed her gently and helped her on with her clothes, and covered her with her coat, and she snuggled into him as they drove back to Chicago. In the inner city, they passed a small, pocket park.

'Want to walk?' said Remo.

'Yes, dear. But we can't here. It's a coloured neighborhood.'

'I think we'll be all right,' he said.

'I don't know,' said Chris, worry on her face.

'Do you trust me, honey?' said Remo.

'You called me "honey," ' said Chris, beaming.

'Do you trust me?'

'Oh, yes, Remo. Yes.'

They walked into the park. It was littered with broken bottles; its trees were scarred; its bushes uprooted, and its jungle gym was bent and cracked. A dark, drunken hulk was sleeping one off under a scarred bench.

Chris smiled and kissed Remo's shoulder. 'This is the most beautiful park I've ever been through. Just smell the air.'

Remo smelled only the drifting odor of garbage dumped from a window because someone didn't bother to walk to a garbage can down the hall.

They sat down on a bench, and Remo wrapped her

with an arm, bringing her warm, close, and secure.

'Darling,' he said sweetly. 'Tell me about yourself and Jethro and the union and the men in those rooms and Nuihc.'

And she talked. She told of how she first met Gene Jethro, and Remo asked when he started having money. She talked about Gene's change in temperament, and Remo asked if Nuihc had supplied the money. She talked about the building outside of the city that took so much of Gene's time, leaving her alone, and Remo asked if she had a key to the building. He noted that it must be hard on someone as sensitive as herself to share a floor with those horrible men. Oh, those men weren't horrible. They were Gene's friends. They were the presidents of the three other unions which would join with Gene's, but Remo knew that already, didn't he?

Yes, Remo did. He even knew they were going to make the joining tomorrow. Those men, however, were unfaithful to their wives. Chris knew that and she knew the wives also. Remo wouldn't be the unfaithful kind, would he? Of course not. Could Remo have made love like that if he didn't love her deeply? By the way, did she know where to reach the wives? Yes, she did. She was also Gene's personal secretary. She was chosen for this because she could file things mentally instead of on paper.

No really? She couldn't do that, could she? Remo would like to see her reel off some things.

And so it went until Remo had the full web, the interlocking arrangements of one union with another, the monetary cement that bound closer than blood and tighter than concrete. Did Remo really love her? Of course he did. What sort of a person did she think he was?

Suddenly, footsteps in the night, scuffling footsteps kicking the broken glass before them. Remo turned around. There were eight, ranging from a youngster with afro and comb still in it, to one in his mid-thirties. Eight men with nothing to do at 1 A.M. on a hot spring night in the inner city.

'Oh, my God,' said Chris.

'Don't worry,' said Remo.

Two of the taller men in undershirts and bell bottoms, with multicolored high-heeled shoes and floppy pimp hats angled over their afros, came close. The others surrounded the white couple. Remo could see the black muscles glint in the street light.

'We out of our lily-white neighborhood tonight, ain't we?' said the man on the left.

'The zoo was closed,' said Remo, 'so we thought we'd drop in here.' He could feel Chris pinch his arm in terror.

'Oh you funny, man. Thank you for the white meat. White meat just love black meat.'

Remo's voice was cold and remorseless. He did not wish to do anything without giving full warning of the consequences.

'You bring it out,' said Remo. 'It's coming off.'

'Wrong, honkey, yours is coming off,' said the one on the left. He flashed a shiny razor. The one on the right had a bowie knife. The older man unveiled a chain. The youngster who couldn't have been more than nine or ten, unveiled an icepick. Remo felt Chris's body grow limp. She had fainted.

'Look. Last chance, fellas. I got nothing against you.'

'You can run, honkey. Leave the white pussy for the black brothers who know what to do with it. She just gonna love it.' He smiled a white-toothed, glinting smile. The smile lasted only a second, and then it was a mass of blood as Remo moved through it with a left hand. The knife on the right went into the air. The chain went around a neck, and suddenly bodies were scurrying, running, fleeing out of the park. The youngster, swinging his pick wildly, suddenly realized he was alone.

'Shit,' he said and waited courageously for the onslaught.

'What are you going to do with that?' asked Remo, pointing to the icepick.

'Gonna cut yo' head off if you don' move back.'

Remo moved back.

The young man was delightfully surprised, yet still suspicious. One of his elders managed enough courage to yell from across the street.

'Get outen there, Skeeter.'

'You' ass get outen heah. I got the honkey. You move, Charlie, you dead.'

'I'm not moving,' said Remo.

'Less yo' has bread.'

'You won't kill me if I give you my money?'

'Gimme,' said the youngster, his hand outstretched.

Remo unfolded a ten-dollar bill.

'All.'

'No,' said Remo.

'You gonna get this in you belly,' Skeeter waved the icepick.

'Ten dollars. Take it or leave it.'

'I take it,' said Skeeter. He folded the bill into his chest pocket and sauntered from the park.

'Thet honkey ain't so tough,' he yelled to his hiding friends. The older man promptly smacked Skeeter in the head, knocking him into a trash can. Another held him down while the third grabbed the ten-dollar bill. They left the youngster bloodied, hanging on to the edge of the trash can.

Chris slept in unconsciousness. Remo went over to the youngster, and stuffed two twenties in his shirt.

'That was pretty stupid going back to those guys with ten bucks,' he said.

The youngster blinked and staggered to his feet.

'Those my bruthas and one's my old man, I think.'

'I'm sorry,' said Remo.

'You white honkey shit, I hate you. Ah'll kill you,' and the youngster went tearing at Remo who sidestepped and walked back to Chris, leaving the kid swinging wildly in the street.

Remo kissed her awake.

'Oh,' she said. 'They took me while I was unconscious.'

'Nobody touched you, honey. It's all right.'

'They didn't take me?'

'No.'

'Oh.'

'C'mon, dear. We've got some phone calls to make and the numbers are in your beautiful file cabinet,' he said and he kissed her forehead.

TWELVE

The wives of the presidents of the three other transportation unions were scattered around Chicago in motels. They had been told their husbands were to be working straight through Friday, April 17. They could reach their husbands by phone, but so secret were the negotiations they were conducting, they could not see them.

The wives had ample spending money and constant surveillance. This according to Chris.

'Gene figured that the chance to whoop it up free of interference from their wives was another strong inducement for them to join with the drivers. He said you'd be surprised how many major decisions were made for minor self-indulgences.'

Remo and Chris sat in the car parked in front of the 'The Happy Day Inn,' which boasted, as did all Happy Day Inns, a big marquee. This one said: 'Welcome Drivers. Truck Stop.'

'I can't see the union chiefs making risky decisions like that for, well, some female companionship.'

'Oh, no,' said Chris. 'Gene knew they wouldn't do it for that reason. They got money personally, plus he gave them good deals, higher guaranteed base salaries for their union members. You know with a national union like that, they don't have to bargain for a wage, they submit it. They've got to get what they want or the country starves.'

'Did he think Congress wouldn't pass a law?'

'Oh, Congress could pass a law. But Congress can't

drive a truck or fly a plane or unload a ship.'

'Why didn't he bring the seafarers' union in on this?'

'He didn't need them. They'd only be more of a burden. They got to bring the stuff in. As Gene explained it, the seafarers are pretty much at the mercy of the dockworkers. The dockworkers go on strike and the seafarers can just go play with themselves. It's the delivery to the heartland of America that counts.'

'And this Nuihc figured it all out.'

'Right. He's a creepy little twirp. But he knows what he's doing.'

'What does he look like?'

'A skinny gook.'

'Oh, great. Now we have it down to a third of the world's population. Stay here. I'm going in.'

'Room 3J,' said Chris.

'I remembered.'

'It's just a precaution. Most people can't remember real good.'

'Thanks,' said Remo.

It was 3 A.M., the night was still and quiet. A floodlight lit the Happy Inn sign, and small orange lights outside each door in the courtyard burned a pungent chemical, obviously to keep away bugs.

Remo found 3J and knocked. A man cradling a long pole—Remo peered closer—no, it was a shotgun, turned the corner and approached him.

'Why are you at that...' the man said and then suddenly was saying no more. The gun clanked to the cement walkway. The door opened. A head awash in a collection of curlers and a sea of cold cream poked out of the open door.

'Mrs. Loffer?'

'Yes.'

'My name is Remo Jones, moral squad, Chicago police.'

'There's no one in here,' said the sleepy woman. 'I'm alone.'

'It's not you, ma'am. It's some bad news about your

husband.

'Can I see your badge?'

Remo reached into his pocket and with his right hand grabbed a half-dollar. With his left, he removed his wallet from his jacket. Then with hands covering the movement, he presented to the woman what appeared to be a wallet open with a shiny badge of some sort. In the dark, it worked.

'Okay. Come in.'

Detective Sergeant Remo Jones told Mrs. Loffer the sad and true story of her husband and underage girls.

'The bastard,' said Mrs. Loffer.

He told her the girls were sick and probably even seduced her husband.

'The bastard,' said Mrs. Loffer.

He told her how the girls were probably being used in some national union manipulation and that her husband should probably not be blamed at all.

'The bastard,' said Mrs. Loffer.

Bluntly, he told her he thought her husband was the victim.

'Bullshit. He's a bastard and he always will be,' said Mrs. Loffer.

If Mr. Loffer would leave town this very morning, Chicago police would drop charges.

'You may, but I won't. The bastard,' said Mrs. Loffer.

By 4.30 A.M. Remo had three angry wives in the back seat of the car. The first wife helped convince the second, and the third was dressed and ready to go before Remo had a chance to explain that it wasn't her husband's fault.

At 4.30 A.M. just outside the city limits in a new building with some of the plaster still drying and the plumbing just beginning to work, Gene Jethro sat beside a pool in an indoor garden listening, nodding, working his hands nervously, and perspiring profusely.

'Can't we just ignore the guy?'

'No,' said the other person in a high, squeaky voice.

'Look. I don't have anything against him. So he walked with Chris. She was just another broad, anyhow.'

'It is not that he has taken your woman. It is not that he is most dangerous. It is that proper precautions indicate he be dead.'

'We used the truck. It didn't work. The guy gives me the creeps, Nuihc.'

'This will work.'

'How do you know?'

'I know what will work on this man. And once he is gone, then the other person will go.'

'Oh, we can take the little gook, I mean Oriental gentleman.'

'Did your three men, as you say it, take the gook?'

'I'm sorry for that expression, sir.'

'Let me tell you something. Neither you nor your men nor your children, given weapons of the utmost ferocity, given coordination beyond your pitiful imagination, could, as you so crudely say it, take that little gook.'

'But he's an old man. He's ready to die.'

'So you say. And so you have lost three men. You think your eyes can tell you truths, when you cannot see. You think your ears can tell you truths, when you cannot hear. You think your hands can tell you truths, when you do not know what it is you feel. You are a fool. And a fool must be told in detail what to do.'

Gene Jethro listened and watched the long fingernails as they made arrows in the air.

'In your Western ambush, you are very blunt. You arrange that weapons begin their assault at the same time. This you think is most effective. It is not, especially against one man who knows the bare rudiments of his craft. Rather a more subtle ambush is in order, two layers of surprises beyond the initial trap. Now, let us take a normal ambush, four sides or three it does not matter. Guns firing here. Guns firing there. And guns firing there. Impossible to escape, right?'

'I guess so, sir,' said Jethro.

'No. Not in the least. With speed one can eliminate one point before the others really become effective. What I'm talking about are fractions of your seconds. But we are assuming our target is not as clumsy as you. So, he destroys a single point and then begins to work on the others or runs or whatever he wills. This sort of ambush works only against amateurs. So, but let us say that each point is an ambush. Let us create firing patterns around each individual firing pattern, and these patterns stay quiet until that point is attacked.'

'It's like doubling the chances,' said Jethro.

'No. It is increasing the effectiveness nine times. Now we're assuming he will attack the points if he has been trained correctly. Remember now, the secondary level does not fire at him originally—only when he attacks the primary level. Secondary must hold its fire. Now you set up a third level for the second level. And you increase your effectiveness, not by nine times, but nine to the ninth power. You use only twenty-seven men. Twenty-seven men for an infinitely large effectiveness than three times three times three.'

'Yeah, but where are we gonna set this thing up? The Mojave desert?'

'Don't be absurd. A hotel is perfect. Perfect. With their rooms and hallways, perfect. The lobby of his hotel. Even you could figure out how that would work.'

'I'm scared.'

'There's this or, if you prefer, a puddle.'

'You need me. You can't do what you do without me.'

'And who were you when I found you? A shop steward. If I can make a shop steward into the Gene Jethro of today, I can do it with anyone. I have taught you to love as no Westerner can love. I have given you a gadget weapon designed for your incompetence that dissolves your worst opponents. I have made you Gene Jethro, and I can do the same for someone else. I do not need you. I use you. I am surprised you have not figured this out by now.'

'But you said you just wanted to help me. You said you saw so much potential in me that it was a shame I was wasting it.'

'A pretty little song for a foolish little head.'

Gene Jethro sighed and stared at a hanging palm, then down at his hands.

'What if this older Oriental gentleman should decide to come here after us, if he's as good as you say.'

'He has been here and left. We need have no worry about that gentleman. He is not a fool.'

'Twenty-seven you say? In his hotel lobby?'

'Correct. Three protected by three, each protected by three.'

'I better get going then.'

'Call your people to you. I'm afraid you're not leaving here.'

'But the convention. The 17th. This is our biggest day.'

'It shall come to pass,' said the man with the flat Oriental voice. 'It shall come to pass. Who would have thought that I could build this structure in two months? Who would have thought I could raise you to a presidency in two months? It shall come to pass, for you see, my friend, it is written both in the stars and in my mind. Our little white adversary whom you fear will be dead before another sun sets. You will be the most powerful labor leader by another sunset. And I shall have what I want.'

'What do you want?'

The flat Oriental face smiled. 'One thing at a time. First the whiteling. Of course, he might escape.'

Nuihc took joy in the sudden shock on the face of his whiteling.

'He could escape this ambush,' said Nuihc.

'But . . .'

'If he knows the scarlet ribbon. But do not add unnecessary worries to your heart. No white man could ever comprehend the scarlet ribbon, any more than you.'

Remo reached Jethro's headquarters hotel. Surprisingly, the entrance was easy. No reinforcements—the door hadn't even been repaired. Chris waited downstairs out of sight in the car parked a few blocks away.

The women climbed the flights of steps, driven by anger and rage, panting, stumbling, pressing forward, mumbling, 'Wait'll I get him.'

They paused on the eighteenth floor. The door was still open at the hinges. Remo opened it wider for the women. They pushed through, panting. When the guard saw Remo, he hurriedly pressed the elevator button. Jumping up and down in fear, he looked nervously at the indicator dial and then back at Remo and the women. The door opened and Remo could see him lunge for the close button. He let him go. The quartet stormed to the far door.

'It's open,' said Remo. 'There was some trouble with the lock breaking. They just don't make things the way they used to.' Snores could be heard from inside.

'That's him,' said Mrs. Loffer. 'I know that snore,' Remo eased the door open. The other women watched. One whispered:

'Cut out his heart.'

Remo followed. Mrs. Loffer stared at the bed, illuminated by a small night light, a middle-aged man with a redhead snuggled in his arms.

'She's a perfect size ten,' sobbed Mrs. Loffer, her voice cracking. 'A perfect size ten.'

She tiptoed to the bed. Remo could smell the nausea of stale champagne. Mrs. Loffer leaned down, close to her husband's ear.

'Joey. Honey. I heard a noise downstairs.'

Still snoring. The redhead turned over, her mouth wide open in a grinding rasp of a nasal symphony.

Mrs. Loffer nudged her husband's hairy shoulder.

'Joey. Honey. It's time for coffee. Go downstairs and get the coffee, honey. Gotta make the coffee.'

Snores. The redhead size ten opened her eyes, saw Remo, saw the woman, and started to scream. Remo had his hand over her mouth before the sound could begin.

Joseph Loffer, leader of the best-paid workers in the world, pilots whose average salary topped $30,000 a year, awoke, presumably to go downstairs to start the coffee.

He opened his eyes, kissed his wife, and suddenly became totally awake when he saw that his wife was dressed, and that a man was holding the mouth of his nude paramour. He was about to launch a desperate explanation when Mrs. Loffer clobbered him. The blow took off from the floor and ended in his testicles. As he doubled over, Mrs. Loffer caught him with a knee in the face, then an open hand slap to the cheek, then fingernails to the eyes. He tumbled back on the bed, Mrs. Loffer on top.

It was not a bad attack at all and Remo wondered at the capacity of some people, whether by instinct or through rage, to execute an almost perfect interior line attack. Of course, there were no fatal blows, but still Mrs. Loffer kept up the unrelenting pressure along the center of her body and Joey's. She sustained well, she executed rather well, and all in all, Remo had to admit she was doing a fine job.

'See if you can get the elbows into it. Very nice, Mrs. Loffer. Very nice. Let me say, for someone without training, superb. That's it, keep up the pressure, very nice. No, no roundhouse blows. You've got a nice interior-line attack going there, and I wouldn't spoil it now,' said Remo.

Mrs. Loffer, tired, rolled off her husband, who lay stunned and bleeding slightly. She sat on the edge of the bed, lowered her head into her hands, and sobbed hysterically. Her husband managed to raise himself on his elbows and then, with a mighty effort, pushed himself to sitting position.

'I'm sorry.' he said. 'I'm sorry.'

'You bastard,' said Mrs. Loffer. 'You bastard. Get packed. We're going.'

'I can't go.'

'You tell that to the policeman. You were doing such awful things, even the morals squad got involved.'

'There's no law, dear...'

'You'll see from my lawyer whether there's a law or not.'

'I can't go.'

Remo released the redhead.

'Better get dressed and out of here,' he said.

She shot him a dirty look.

'You're a private detective, aren't you?'

'Get dressed,' he said. 'And you, Mr. Loffer, I want you dressed and out of this city in half an hour.'

Remo took the next wife to the center room. She emptied two ashtrays on the pile of bodies and hit every limb, buttock, and face her nails could reach. Her husband cowered in the corner. Remo threw him his clothes.

'Be out of Chicago in a half hour or you're in jail.'

The third room was less of a battle. The wife burst into tears when she saw her husband entangled in a melange of female parts. She put her head into Remo's chest and began to cry. A tingle of guilt crossed Remo's emotions. Yet, it was either get them out of town or between a beam. The nation could not survive what they were about to do to it.

This husband was furious. How dare his wife break in on him? How dare his wife have him followed? How dare his wife not trust him?

Remo explained that the husband was violating a morals ordinance, which Remo conveniently made up. Granted, the ordinance was written in 1887, but it still holds true today, as it did when the Chicago forefathers passed it unanimously.

'Yeah. Well, it ain't constitutional,' said the president of the dockworkers. 'I can get it thrown out of court.'

'You're going to fight it in the courts?'

'You're damned right I am.'

The president of the International Stevedores Association had a very interesting lower right rib. Remo readjusted it. The gentleman, amid a loud wail, reconsidered his legal course and agreed to get out of Chicago.

There was a mass exodus from the hotel that morning as the first faint red lines appeared in the gray Chicago sky. First the ladies of the evening. Then, the husbands and wives. But Remo, leaning against a lampost, waiting to make sure, was not really sure at all as he saw the last husband engage the attention of the other couples. At the end of the block they flagged down a squad car. The two other husbands and all the women suddenly pretended they did not know this man, as he spoke to the two policemen in the squad car.

When Remo saw the driver laugh, he knew his little ploy had been shot. The third man had not been panicked by the situation. He had kept his head. Checked out an ordinance. Found out it was nonexistent, and through his coolness of action was going to get himself and his companions killed today – a beam would go hurtling down on a row of union delegates who knew no such morals law had been passed in 1887. Unanimously. The way they would have to die.

It was a bad report for Smith. Extreme actions are to be used when you have lost everything else. Only fools, madmen, and losers resort to them. As Remo ducked out of sight, he knew he was in the latter category.

THIRTEEN

The plan was simple. And it was safe.

Rocco Pigarello explained it again to the twenty-six other men. He wasn't asking anyone to get killed. He wasn't asking anyone to commit murder. He was asking the men merely to make some money. He wasn't even going to mention that these men were the least important in the entire union because they were muscle and muscle could be bought cheap anytime. No. He wasn't going to mention unpleasant things because he had a very pleasant proposition and he did not wish to mar its sweetness.

'What I want from you guys is a little common sense and thay you should defend yourselves if attacked or if anyone attacks one of your driver brothers. Right?'

A few suspicious mumbles of 'right,' 'yeah,' and 'okay' emanated from the twenty-six men sitting sullenly sleepily in the large auditorium that smelled of fresh paint. They had been awakened in the motel rooms and hotel rooms in the wee hours and hustled to this new building just outside Chicago. In some cases it was the president of the local who woke them. In others it was another delegate or a business agent. It was always someone in direct command over them. And they were not *asked* to get up early, they were *told* to do so. Or else.

As soon as the auditorium started filling, the men recognized each other. Muscle. From Dallas, San Francisco, Columbus, Savannah. Twenty-six men with special reps. They saw each other and they knew there would be blood, and they didn't like it because this convention was to be one of their rewards for loyal service, not some more work.

The Pig continued. 'I know many of you guys think it unfair to bring you here at this hour. I know many of you guys think you ought to be back asleep. But let me tell you, you're here because ... because....' Pigarello thought a moment. 'Because you're here.'

Angry mumbling from the men.

'Now I am asking you to protect a brother driver. I am asking you to protect a fellow union member from vicious goons. I'm gonna tell you all your places. If you see anyone attacking a fellow driver, shoot him in defense of that fellow driver. We have the lawyers ready and we foresee no trouble. No trouble, okay.'

Angry mumbles.

'Now, it is my suspicion that this company goon, this strong-arm man, will attack me with a pistol. I am sure all of you will see this. You will see the attack with the pistol. Once you hear a shot, it will mean he has begun to attack a brother driver. You will defend that brother driver. This is the picture of the man I expect to attack me.' The Pig raised a glossy, magazine-sized photograph above his head.

A few mumbles of shock. The recording secretary. They were going to do a job on the recording secretary.

'Now. Any questions?'

A delegate from a Wyoming local rose. He was as tall and lean and rawboned as his cowboy ancestors.

'How many men is that gentleman going to bring? I mean we have twenty-seven men, Pig, and I don't hanker to go up against no fifty or a hundred of Abe Bludner's boys.'

'Bludner is on our side,' said the Pig.

Mumbles of approval.

'You mean to say, this Remo Jones is going up against you without his president's approval?' asked the Wyoming delegate.

'You heard me.'

'Where's he getting his support?'

'He ain't got none.'

'You mean to tell me he's all alone and he's going up against you, Pig?'

'Yeah.'

'I don't rightly believe that.'

'Yeah, well you better rightly believe it, shitkicker, because this guy is gonna do just that. Now sit down. Any more questions?'

Three hands raised.

'Take 'em down,' said the Pig. 'Questions are over.'

Remo hailed a cab.

'How much time do you have left on your shift?' he asked.

The cabby looked puzzled.

'How much time are you willing to work today?'

The driver shrugged. 'Usually people ask are you willing to go this far or that far, not how much time.'

'Well I'm not usual people and I've got some unusual money.'

'Look, I've had a good day. I'm not interested in anything shady.'

'Nothing shady. You want to earn twelve hours?'

'I'm beat.'

'A hundred dollars.'

'I feel refreshed.'

'Good. Just drive this lady around Chicago for twelve hours and don't stop for more than ten minutes anywhere.'

Remo eased Chris into the back of the cab.

'Honey. You get your rest right here in the back of the cab,' he said. He ostentatiously handed Chris a wad of bills, letting the driver know there was money to be paid.

'But why can't I go to your hotel with you, darling?' said Chris.

Remo whispered in her ear. 'Because we're marked

people. You're a target. I'd bet on it. I'll meet you at O'Hare International Airport at six or seven tonight. The bar is the best restaurant. Whatever it is. If I'm not there, wait until midnight. If I don't come, run for your life. Change your name and keep going. In two days stop.'

'Why two days?'

'Because it's been worked out that two days is an ideal time in a run pattern like this, and I don't have time to explain.

'Why can't I just book a six-hour flight out and a six-hour flight back if you want me to keep traveling for twelve hours?'

'Because a scheduled flight is like an elevator. In something like this it functions like a stationary room that keeps you locked in. Take my word. This is best.'

'I'm not afraid of Gene, darling.'

'I am. Move.' Remo kissed Chris on the cheek and nodded to the cab driver. He made obvious a check of the cabbie's identification, not that he would remember it. He just wanted the man to believe that he would be remembered and vulnerable if anything should happen to the girl.

April 17 was a hot day in Chicago, the muggy, skin-soaking kind of morning that makes you feel you've worked a full day when you get up. Remo hadn't slept. He could make do with twenty minutes rather easily, and with this intention he headed back to his hotel.

He did not get rest. As he entered the marble-floored lobby, he saw a man ease a rifle barrel in his direction. Automatically he did not respond to this man who had taken the rifle out of a golf bag leaning against a lobby sofa. As he had been trained to do, he first checked—in an instant—the entire pattern he was in. Other guns came out. From suitcases, from a carton, from behind the registration clerk's desk. Ambush.

Remo would work it left to right. Not bothering to feint, he was into a rugged man who was squeezing the trigger on a Mauser. The Mauser did not fire. It was jammed up into the solar plexus, taking part of a lung with it. The man vomited his lungs, and Remo continued to work right so that his being in the right firing pattern prevented the center and left from getting him without shooting into their own men.

A woman screamed. A porter jumped for cover, catching a wayward bullet in the throat. Two young children huddled against a sofa. Remo would have to work the line of fire away from the children. But if he could not, whoever might have fired the shots that injured the youngsters would not die quickly.

The right side was too bunched. Amateurs. Remo thumbed a side of a head, and interior-attacked a thin man with a .357 Magnum. It was held too close to the body, as though the man were working a snub-nose at close quarters. The trigger finger was squeezing off a shot so the gun went first. With a wrist. Then the head caved in and Remo was moving towards the center, going under a rifle line to come up under it when a shot cracked passed his head. He felt it in his hair.

Double layer. Remo finished the driver through the rifleman, taking off his testicles. The man would be stunned until dead. He spun back to where the second level of fire came from, another bullet narrowly missing him from the center. He was now in cross fire. Very stupid move on his part.

He quickly put a post between him and center left, taking that line into the dining room, whence the second-level fire came.

They were using tables here as cover. One man got a table top, tablecloth and all, in his mouth. Down through a vertebra. A nervous, wildly chattering machine gun ended its chirp with the barrel in its user's mouth, still firing from a trigger finger that could no longer receive messages to stop. The bullets took skull fragments and brain into the ceiling.

Remo's body wove and jerk-ran into a free space that

suddenly had a bullet in it, taking flesh from Remo's right side. Minor wound.

Without thinking, Remo reacted. His body reacted as it had been taught to react in the painful, pressing hours of training, reacted as Chiun had taught it despite Remo's protests, despite Remo's conscious begging for surcease, despite the long hours and high temperatures.

As it had been taught and no other way. Scarlet Ribbon for the three times three times three. It was not only the *only* defense, but against this combination it was invincible. Back toward the center he moved, keeping lines of fire within the ambush itself. He did not attack men anymore because that would remove them, and the Ribbon depended upon the men to destroy themselves, like using the greater mass of a body against itself.

He brushed the center and spun back, careful not to let any close shots, which were the easiest to avoid, get him. The distant, more dangerous, shots were now no worry because there would be other men in their line.

With incredible, balanced speed, Remo, like a darting flash of light brought down from the heavens, spun his ribbon in the three-layered defense. Guns silenced when the speeding body disappeared among other men of the ambush, then resumed in the fleeting second he was visible. Wild shots. Hesitant shots. The target was no longer the center of the ambush. The target was part of it.

Through the registration desk, back up through the triple layer left, over the staircase, keeping close and unhittable to the confused and now panicked men, Remo worked to third layer center, second layer center, picked off a first layer center only for the rebound back to third layer right.

Bullets cracked into light fixtures spraying the lobby with a shower of glass. Mindless screaming and yelling whipped the panic still further. An elevator door opened and a maid was cut in two by a shotgun blast. On the final spin of the ribbon, Remo took care of the man who fired the shotgun. He creased the man's eyes with his fingernails, leaving two blood-gushing sockets in the skull.

Then fast up the middle, picking up the two children from the couch, then a reverse into the dining room, out again and behind the third layer that did not know he had penetrated up the steps, and wait. Standing on the steps, waiting. The gunfire continued. The two children stared at him, confused.

What had happened was natural. Instead of acting like professionals, the men in the parts of the ambush catching fire, returned it. The men were fighting for their lives *against each other*. The Scarlet Ribbon had woven the blood curse of fear and confusion into the ambush. It would never recover. If Remo wished, he could wait to the last spurts of firing, and move in for the final kill. But that was not his purpose. The only thing he wanted from the ambush was to get through it alive.

The little girl looked stunned. The boy was smiling.

'Bang, bang,' said the boy. 'Bang, bang.'

'Your mommy and daddy around here?' asked Remo.

'They're on the third floor. They told us to play in the lobby.'

'Well you go back up to your parents' room.'

'They said we shouldn't come back until 9.30,' said the girl.

'Bang, bang,' said the boy.

'You can't go downstairs again.'

Rifle fire cracked sporadically in the hallway. Sounds of far-off sirens could be heard filtering into the stairway where Remo stood with the two children.

'All right. But would you come with us?' said the girl.

'I'll come with you.'

'And tell my mommy and daddy that we can't play in the lobby.'

'I'll do that.'

'And tell them we didn't do the trouble downstairs.'

'I'll do that.'

'And give us a dollar.'

'Why give you a dollar?'

'Well, a dollar would be nice, too.'

'I'll give you a quarter,' said Remo. 'A nice shiny quarter.'

'I'd rather have a dirty old dollar.'

Remo brought the two youngsters to their parents' room. His shirt was bloody and his pants were beginning to darken. It was uncomfortable, but not serious.

The father opened the door. He was bleary-eyed, a face of anguish, a face of alcohol-damaged brain cells, the damaging process of which was pleasant, and the results painful.

'What trouble did you kids cause now?'

'They didn't cause any trouble, sir. Some madmen went amok with guns downstairs, and your children might have been killed.'

'I didn't know,' said the man. He tied the terrycloth belt around his terrycloth robe. 'Are they all right? Are you all right?'

'Yes. I got nicked. You know us innocent passersby. Always getting hurt.'

'Terrible what's happening to America these days. Is it safe to go downstairs?'

Remo listened. The gunfire had stopped. The police were probably flooding the lobby now. The sirens were about that much time away when he first heard them.

'Yes. But I'd advise you to go back to sleep. It's not a pretty sight.'

'Yeah, thanks. C'mon in, kids.'

'Bang, bang,' said the little boy.

'Shut up,' said the father.

'What is it dear?' came a woman's voice.

'Some trouble in the lobby'.

'Those kids are gonna get it,' yelled the woman.

'Not their fault,' said the father shutting the door.

Remo walked up the flights to his floor. The blood flow was stemming now, coagulating as it should. The shirt became sticky. When he entered the suite, Chiun was asleep by the window, lying on his floor mat, curled like a fetus in peaceful repose, his face to the window.

'You're wounded,' he said without turning around. without the twitch of body to indicate awakeness. He was sleeping and his mind registered sounds, and he was quietly awake in an instant, trained since childhood to awake immediately upon the entrance of a strange sound and trained to awake in such a manner as to avoid giving any indications that he was awake. It was many of the little advantages that made up the Master of Sinanju, supreme teacher of the martial arts, respected leader of the small Korean village that depended on his rented services for its financial survival.

'Not serious,' said Remo.

'Every wound is serious. A sneeze is serious. Wash it clean and rest.'

'Yes, little father.'

'How did it go?'

'Not too well.'

'It went well enough. I felt vibrations of rifle fire through the floor.'

'Oh that. Yeah it was a three, three, three that took a Scarlet Ribbon.'

'Why are you wounded?'

'I started the Ribbon late.'

'Never before,' said Chiun, 'has so much been given to so few who used it so little. I might as well give my instructions to walls as to a white man.'

'All right. All right. I'm wounded. Lay off.'

'Wounded. A minor flesh wound, and we make it into the great tragedy. We have more important problems. You must rest. We will flee soon.'

'Run?'

'That is the usual word in the English language for run, is it not?'

'I can't go, Chiun. I have work. We can't run.'

'You are talking silliness and I am trying to rest.'

'What happened at the building, Chiun?' Remo asked.

'What happened at the building is why we must run.'

Dr. Harold Smith got the report late in the morning, at 10.12. The phone line was activated ever hour at twelve minutes past the hour. From 6 A.M. Eastern Standard Time until 6 P.M. Eastern Standard Time, this was done with direct link to Smith. If he were not in his office, a tape recording would be accepted. Into this tape recording Remo would read the message as best he could in medical terms. Thus, if the message were discovered by others, it would only be a doctor reading in an odd hour report.

At 10.12 when the buzzer on his phone rang, Smith knew from the very first words that the plan would be the extreme one.

'My alternate plan didn't work,' came Remo's voice.

'All right,' said Dr. Smith. 'You know what to do.'

'Yeah.'

And that was it. The phone was dead, and four of the nation's leading labor leaders were going to die.

'Damn,' said Dr. Smith. 'Damn.'

If the system could not tolerate collective bargaining, then maybe the American system was just false. Maybe the patch-up work CURE did only delayed the final outcome. Maybe business and labor were supposed to function as warring, hostile giants, with the public whipsawed in between. After all, Dr. Smith knew, business had a history of doing just what the unions were trying to do now. It was called cornering the market, and that was considered the height of business acumen. Why should the unions not be allowed to do the same?

Dr. Smith spun to view Long Island Sound, deep and green and going far out into the Atlantic. Perhaps there should be a sign, 'You are leaving the Sound. Now entering the Atlantic.' But there were no signs, either on the Sound or in life. It was wrong for the unions to blackmail the nation like this, just as it was wrong for businessmen to corner the market in a certain commodity and drive up its prices. He must begin to work the agency towards stopping that sort of crime. And so, staring at Long Island Sound, Dr. Harold Smith planned to enact a piece of American legislation. Without votes. Without writing. Without immediate public knowledge. But he would enact it somehow, someday: it would be illegal for corporations to corner the market and drive up the price of food. And he would not stop at using 'The Destroyer,' just as he had not hesitated to use him today.

FOURTEEN

Remo slipped the wrapped crowbar with Bludner's fingerprints on it into the back of his pants. Then he put his shirt over it, and a jacket over that. He surrounded the crowbar with muscle, cushioning it between his shoulder blades, keeping the metal rod positioned on top and hidden behind the jacket. The forked end of the crowbar nestled right behind his reproductive organs, following the curve of his body. An X-ray would have shown a man sitting on a curved bar.

A good tap on his back would, Remo knew, cause him great pain. He walked somewhat stiffly to the door of his hotel suite.

'I'll be back.'

'You are going to that building?' Chiun said in caution.

'No,' said Remo.

'Good. When you return I will tell you why we must run. If I did not have to stay here and watch over an impetuous youth,' said Chiun. 'I would leave now. It is no matter, however. We will leave later, after you expend your wasted energy.'

'It will not be wasted, little father.'

'It will be wasted, but feel free to indulge yourself. Amuse yourself.'

'This is not amusement, little father.'

'It is not work, Remo. It is not productive, mature work.'

'I am going to set things right which must be set right.'

'You are going to indulge yourself in wasted effort. Goodnight.'

Remo exhaled his frustration. One did not reason with Chiun. For all his wisdom he could not know the threat of four unions joining into one. For all his wisdom he was wrong this morning.

The lobby was aswarm with police, newspapermen, photographers, TV cameras. The ambulance drivers had left, most of them headed for morgues.

Rocco 'the Pig' Pigarello was perspiring under the television lights. His arm was bandaged, undoubtedly the result of a bullet from one of his own men.

'Yeah. These crazy men were shooting at us for no reason. It was an assault against organized labor by gangsters.'

'Mr. Pigarello, police say all the injured and dead were union men.' The newscaster held a microphone to Pigarello's face.

'Dat's right. We had no way to defend ourselves. There must have been twenty, maybe thirty wid guns.'

'Thank you, Mr. Pigarello,' said the television newscaster. He turned to his cameraman.

'That was Rocco Pigarello, a delegate to the International Brotherhood of Drivers' convention here in Chicago, a union that has been severely hurt today in an outburst of senseless violence.'

Remo watched Pigarello's eyes. They spotted him. The Pig went to a police captain. He shot Remo a furtive glance. Remo smiled at the Pig. The Pig suddenly forgot what he was going to say to the captain, and Remo walked from the hotel out into the busy morning street through a corridor of police barricades. People gawked over the barricades, they leaned from windows across the street, they stood on tiptoes on the opposite sidewalk.

A bright blue Illinois sky covered it all—with, of course, a layer of air pollution sandwiched in between. Remo hailed a cab to the convention hall.

The driver talked about the horrible killings in the

hotel, how Chicago wasn't safe anymore, and how everything would be fine if only the Blacks left Chicago.

'Blacks weren't involved,' said Remo.

'So in this one incident,' said the driver, 'they weren't involved. Don't tell me that if we didn't have coloreds the crime rate wouldn't drop.'

'It would drop even faster if we didn't have people,' said Remo.

The convention hall was, strangely, all but deserted. No uniformed guards to take delegates' tickets, no vendors preparing for special bars with the early tubs of ice, no last-minute scurrying of workers giving the microphone system a last-minute check. No one was even placing the day's agenda on the seats as they had done every day since Monday.

Even the gates were locked. At the third gate, Remo decided to stop looking for someone to let him in. He walked in, right through the crowdproof, locked gate. His footsteps echoed down the dark, deserted corridors that smelled freshly cleaned. The stands exuded a faint yesterday's-beer odor. The air was cool yet without freshness. A lone worker stood on a ladder installing a light bulb. Remo stayed in the shadows enough not to be recognized but not enough to appear suspicious.

'Hi,' Remo said, walking on as though he belonged in the deserted corridor.

'Hi,' said the workman.

Remo scampered up to the top tier and paused. He was two aisles away. The banner was still and flat.

'Welcome, International Brotherhood of Drivers.' Not a ripple. The crowds would change that. The body heat would change that. Yet even with no one inside the huge structure, it should get some air currents. Perhaps too many doors and windows were closed on the outside. Remo ducked back into the corridor and came out perfect. Fifty feet above him was the joint of the beam that stretched across the huge dome of the hall. He eased the crowbar from the back of his pants with the protective paper still on it. An edge of the paper was smeared with his blood. The wound had coagulated, but apparently not fast enough to keep the paper dry. He checked the crowbar, looking for the glistening hint of his own blood. He did not want blood on the crowbar to complicate things. It should be a very simple crime. Abe 'Crowbar' Bludner had somehow unriveted the beam and was stupid enough to leave the crowbar. The police, desperately in need of a suspect for the murder of four union officials, would gratefully and rapidly pick Bludner. Blood would be a minor complication that might set their minds to working on other angles. Not that he would be implicated, but as Chiun had said, fools and children take chances.

'It is the height of arrogance to fling your chances of survival into the lap of the goddess of fate, demanding that she perform what you will not. This arrogance is always punished.'

Remo eased out of his shoes. He rewrapped the crowbar. There was no blood. He leaped to a small overhang and held with one hand. Working with feet forward and one hand behind it, he slithered up the curved wall. His free hand was used as a foot now because two feet were better for grabbing than one free hand. In the other hand was the evidence against Bludner.

Suddenly walking sounds, hollow, leather, clicking walking sounds came towards him. Two men. Remo pressed against the wall. His blood rushing headward, but unlike ordinary men he could sustain this pressure and function for three hours.

'Hey, Johnny. One of those idiot driver delegates left his shoes.'

'They should have been picked up by cleaning. That contractor we use is getting sloppy. I mean it. Sloppy. You never should have hired him.'

'What's this "you" jazz? We both hired him.'

'You recommended him.'

'And you said "Okay."'

'I said "Okay" because you recommended him. I'm not

going to listen to your recommendations anymore.'

They stood directly beneath Remo, a bald head and a grease conglomerate swirled in such a way as to hide impending departure of hair. This was very evident to anyone who wanted to cling upside down directly above a grease-coated head.

'I recommended the drivers. You want to give back their money?'

'So one of your recommendations finally turns out all right. What do you want, a medal?'

'I want a little appreciation. You know any other outfit that would pay for a place like this on a day they're not using it?'

'Yeah, anyone else who signed a contract and at three in the morning said they weren't going to use the place that day.'

'They could hold up the final payment. They could talk deal. They could talk settlement. The people I rent to pay in full, anyway.'

'When you rented at the last minute, I was the one who told you to go ahead. I was the one who, with two pathetic months, broke the contract for that horse show.'

'Because I got you the drivers, dumbell. For the drivers I'd break a contract with God.'

'For five cents you'd break a contract with God. He could fall down right now and you'd break a contract for five cents.'

It was as good a time as any to collect his shoes. The drivers would not be meeting in the giant hall that day, and there was no point getting Abe Bludner indicted for murdering a circus or a basketbell team or whoever was there when the vibrations, unaided by Remo, would determine that the beam would fall.

Remo dropped gently, missing the greasy head.

'My shoes, please,' said Remo indignantly. He grabbed the shoes from the startled men and handed the greasy-headed one the paper-wrapped crowbar. The paper was still flecked with blood.

'And here's your crowbar. You shouldn't leave it lying around. People could trip over it and get hurt.'

'On the ceiling?' asked the bewildered men.

Remo slipped into his shoes. 'Anywhere,' said Remo. 'Carelessness cannot be excused.'

And with that he was back into his shoes and walking briskly down a corridor towards anything that resembled an exit. He had wasted his effort, as Chiun had said he would. The crowbar would not be needed now. It was as useless as the Maginot Line. Besides, one didn't need a crowbar when one was going to die.

Gene Jethro listened as the Pig, his arm getting a fresh bandage from Sigmund Negronski, explained how it had all happened. The Pig was awash in sweat despite the even chill of the air-conditioned basement of the new building.

'I had it set good. In the lobby like you told me. Twenty-seven guys including me. I was in your third layer central. The first layer was in the lobby or facing it like we planned. You know, rooms surrounding the lobby and the stairs we used for first layer and beginning of second. And the third, I placed it myself because I was in it. I mean I was really careful. The registration desk, I had a guy behind. I had 'em waiting just right, and the guns concealed and every man knew what he was supposed to do. The first layer was the dining room right, the registration clerk center and the ...'

'Go on. Go on,' said Jethro.

Negronski gently taped the bandage and eyed Jethro. The smiling confidence was no longer there. The joyous manipulation of men was no longer in the face grown suddenly old. Deep lines clouded his face. He worked a white handkerchief in his hands. He was wearing yesterday's clothes. He had not changed them. Negronski took both joy and pity in Jethro's condition. He fervently wished that they could return to the Nashville local and wrestle with pensions, threatened layoffs, and jurisdictional disputes. A jurisdictional dispute would be good now. Of jurisdictional disputes, he knew. This was all strange.

'Okay,' said the Pig. 'So I got Connor up close to the door as the first layer right. He would fire the first shot. And he's good. He hunts a lot and you know his rep. Like he's made of bones. He's the best man for that first . . .'

'Get to it. Get to it, dammit,' said Jethro.

'Connor misses. He's three feet from the guy and he misses. The first time in his life and he misses. Bang. And nothing. This Remo creep moves like he ain't even been touched. Good-bye, Connor. Like three feet and . . .'

'Dammit, Pig. Get on with it.'

'Then he goes through the first layer right, and he's into and partially through the second layer, and fast. I mean you think you know fast. You think you've seen fast. You think Gale Sayers is fast. Gale Sayers is a cripple. Bob Hayes is a slug. And shifty? Willie Pep is a plodder. Muhammad Ali walks on his heels.'

'Get on with it, Pig!'

'Okay, okay. I'm telling ya what went wrong.'

'You're telling me why you're not responsible for what went wrong, not what went wrong.'

'I did what ya told me.'

'Go on. Go on, damn you.'

'Yeah, well, okay. Then he starts to really move. I mean move. Sometimes you don't see him, he's so fast. I swear on my mother's grave, you don't see him he's moving so fast. And I try to get off a shot. Other guys try to get off shots, and pretty soon we're shooting back at the people who are shooting at us. And then we're in a firefight with ourselves and we don't even see this guy Remo get away.'

'That's what I thought, Pig.'

'It wasn't our fault, Mr. Jethro. Honest.'

Jethro sulked. He turned away from Negronski and Pigarello. He twisted the handkerchief, looked at it a moment, then threw it into a wastebasket.

'You're going to have to wait here, Pig.'

'You ain't gonna do a job on me, are you?'

'No. No. I don't think so.'

'Whadya mean ya don't think so? I mean what is that? You don't think you're gonna kill me. I mean, what is that?'

'That, my dear fat New England friend, is where it is at.'

'You ain't gonna kill me, you shitkicker,' said the Pig. He grabbed a chair. 'You've had it, pretty boy. We ain't in your little room now, Shitkicker. You get yours now. I seen what McCulloch did to you before he went into that room, and you ain't in that room now.' The Pig advanced on Jethro and Negronski went for the chair. With massive, hairy arms the Pig flipped Negronski aside.

'Stay out of this, Siggy. This is me and Jethro.'

Like a lumbering truckload of gravel, Pigarello moved on Jethro, the heavy oak chair raised above his head as if it were light as matchsticks. Negronski raised himself and saw the chair move towards Jethro's head.

But Jethro was standing in a strange position, not like when they'd have to face an occasional challenge in a Nashville bar, but like a peculiar old man with a spine injury. The toes were pointed in. The hands outstretched and curved loosely. The wrists stiff. The face impassive and free of hate, as though listening to a column of tax figures.

The Pig put his bulk into the downward swing of the chair, but Jethro was no longer there. His left hand, with the light-quickness of a laser, was into the Pig's stomach. The chair tumbled harmlessly behind Jethro. The Pig stood as if watching a surprise party for a ghost. The mouth was open. The eyes were popping wide, and his hands dropped to his sides.

Jethro brought what looked to be a dainty slap to the Pig's head. It was like touching a blood faucet. The Pig spit a stream of red. Like a bowling pin, he began to wobble straight-legged, then down, face forward. Crack. Negronski heard the head hit, and shuddered.

'I had to do it, Siggy,' said Jethro.

'You want me to get a doctor down here?' Negronski's voice was flat.

'No. He's dead, Siggy.'

'I guess we're going to have to move him to that special room.'

'Yeah,' said Jethro.

'We ought to have rollers to that room and a regular conveyer belt.'

'What do you mean by that?'

'You know what I mean. You know the Pig isn't the last. You know that room is gonna be filled every week. You know it's never going to end, Gene.'

'No. It will. It will. As soon as we get the transportation lock on the country, we'll be home free. Everything will quiet down then. It'll be beautiful, Siggy. Beautiful.'

'It'll be more of this,' said Negronski, absently reaching over to the fallen Pigarello and straightening the bandage, for reasons beyond his comprehension. 'It was supposed to be beautiful when we got the convention switched to Chicago. It was supposed to be beautiful when we got the building built. It was supposed to be beautiful when you become president of the drivers. Yeah. And the only thing we got was more killing and more bodies, and more of that room over there. It's never gonna end, Gene. Let's give up and go home. I wouldn't even mind doing time now. Going to the cops, leveling the whole thing. There's no death penalty anymore. And I don't think we'd get the chair anyhow even if there was. Give a full confession. Maybe we'd spend most of the rest of our lives in jail, but it would be our lives. Not running to kill this guy because of this, or that guy because of that. It never ends, Gene. What do you say. For old times' sake. Let's chuck this thing.'

'We can't,' said Jethro. 'Help me with the body.'

'It used to be Pigarello. He's not just a body.'

'It's a body, Siggy. And it's either our bodies or his body. Now which do you want it to be?'

'Nobody, Gene. I'm through.' Sigmund Negronski rose to his full height. His legs planted firm, he stared the new president of the International Brotherhood of Drivers directly in the eye.

'I'm through, Gene. No more. Maybe you can't stop. Maybe you can't get out, but I can. I quit. Right now I wouldn't even touch a sparrow if it were pecking at my head. I'd run. And right now, I'm running. I'm through. I helped you. I stepped aside for you. I helped you, but I'm not helping you anymore. I'm not gonna talk to the police because I know you'd kill me, Gene. That's the way it is nowadays, and I want to live. I want to see tomorrow so bad I can breathe the morning already. Back home. Not here in Chicago. I want to wake up with my wife next to me with her cold cream and curlers and bitching for me to make the coffee, and I want to worry about getting up the mortgage money, not the body counts. I want to walk down the street and be happy to see people, not happy to not see them, if you know what I mean. I want to live and you can take this union and shove it up your velvet bell bottoms. Good-bye. I'm going back to driving a truck. I'm good at that.'

'Siggy, before you go, help me with this,' said Jethro. His voice was cold and smooth like an ice pond.

'No,' said Negronski.

'Just to the room and then you're through,' Jethro smiled the old smile again, the smile that washed away worries and used to make the business fun.

'Okay. Just to the room.'

When Gene Jethro left the special room an hour later, there were two giant green Garby Bags sitting by the door with a note to the janitor to dump them in the building's furnace. Jethro left the room alone.

FIFTEEN

'I have failed, little father.'

Remo said this mournfully, daring to interrupt Chiun who sat before the hotel television set, entranced by the problems of a housewife telling all to her psychiatrist. Remo knew Chiun had heard him enter. He was on his way to change his clothes when Chiun did something Remo had never seen him do before. He turned off the picture on the television. Voluntarily—by himself.

He beckoned Remo to him, turning in his seated position to an empty space on the floor. It was a gesture used by countless Korean teachers of previous generations to students who were to listen to something of great import. It was a gesture of a priest to a neophyte.

Remo sat down on the carpeting facing Chiun, his legs crossed beneath him in the position taught him many years before when just a few minutes of sitting like this would bring excruciating back pains. Now Remo could sleep with his legs tucked under him, his back straight, and awake refreshed.

He looked into the wise, untelling eyes of the man he had first hated, then feared, then respected and finally loved, a father for a man who had known no father, a father for the creation of a new man.

'You know the story of Sinanju, the village of my birth, the village of my father and my father's father and his father before him; of our poverty, of our babies for whom there was naught to eat and who during times of famine would be sent home in the cold waters to return to the larger womb of the sea.

'This then, Remo, you know. You know how the sons must support the village through their knowledge of the martial arts. You know that my monies are shipped to my village. You know how poor the land is there, and that our only resource is the strength of our sons.'

Remo nodded respectfully.

'This you know. But you do not know all. You know I am the Master of Sinanju, but if I am the master, then who is the student?'

'I, little father, am the student,' said Remo.

'I was the Master of Sinanju before you were born.'

'Then there is someone else.'

'Yes, Remo. When I approached that building, the building you could not penetrate, I suspected that you could not penetrate it because if was designed to stop approaches with which you are familiar. When I saw the name of the road leading to the building, I knew who had ordered the construction of that building. I knew there was great danger in there.'

'For me, little father?'

'Especially for you. Why do I of such age have such ease in taking you when we practice, despite your death lunges?'

'Because you are the greatest, little father.'

'Besides that obvious fact.'

'I'm not sure. I guess you know me.'

'Correct. I have taught you all the moves you know. I know what you will do. It is like fighting myself as a young man. I know what you will do before you know what you will do. There is someone else who knows what you will do, and he knows this because I taught him. He has trained since birth, and I have not seen his name until I read a sign leading to that building. Then I needed to know no more. The man you face betrayed his calling and his village. The man who can destroy you is named Nuihc, as the road is named.'

'I've heard that name from one of the sources I used.'

'True. If you reverse the letters you will see that his name and mine are the same.'

'He reversed his name?'

'No. I did. This man, the son of my brother, left his village and plied the craft we taught him, and did not return the sustenance to the people who needed him. In shame before my villagers, I, a teacher, reversed my family name, and left my teaching for service abroad. After me, there is no master of Sinanju. After me, there is no one to support the village. After me, starvation.'

'I am sorry to hear that, little father.'

'Do not be. I have found a student. I have found the new Master of Sinanju to take my place on the day I return home to the womb waters separating China from Korea upon which Sinanju sits like a blessed pearl.'

'That is a great honor, little father.'

'You will be worthy if you do not allow your arrogance and laziness and impure habits to destroy the magnificence of the progress I have initiated and nurtured.'

'Your success but my failure, little father,' said Remo smiling. 'Don't I get a chance to do anything right?'

'When you will have a pupil you will do everything right,' said Chiun with ever so slight a smile, giving himself full approval for a witticism he was sure deserved it.

'This Nuihc. How do I rate next to him?'

Chiun lifted his fingers and closed them to a hair's breadth.

'You are that far away,' he said.

'Good,' said Remo. 'Then I'm in the ball game.'

Chiun shook his head. 'A close second is not a desirable place to finish in a battle to the death.'

'It doesn't have to be a second. I could work something.'

'My son, in five years, you will be this much,' said Chiun, holding his hands a half-foot apart, 'better than he. You must be an aberration of your white race. But this is truth. In five years Nuihc, the ingrate and deserter, will be second place. In five years, I unleash you against the son of my brother and we will bring his kimono back to Sinanju in triumph. In five years there will be no parallel to you. In five years you will surpass even my greatest ancestors. Thus it is written. Thus it is becoming.'

Chiun's voice echoed with pride. Lest his pupil indulge in the vanities to which he was so addicted, Chiun added another thought.

'Thus have I made greatness from nothing.'

'Little father,' said Remo. 'I don't have five years. My country does not have five years. It has until this afternoon.'

'It is a big country. So today one group robs it instead of another. It will be here tomorrow, rich and fat. What is your country to you? Your country executed you. Your country forced you into a life you did not seek. Your country unjustly accused you of a crime.'

'America is my Sinanju, little father.'

Chiun bowed gravely. 'This I understand. But if my village had wronged me as you have been wronged, I would not be its master.'

'A mother cannot wrong a son . . .'

'That is untrue, Remo.'

'I did not finish. A mother cannot wrong a son to such a degree that he will not save her in time of danger. If you are the father I never had, then this nation is the mother I never had.'

'Then in five years give your mother a present of Nuihc's kimono.'

'She must have it now. Come with me. The two of us can surely overcome this Nuihc.'

'Ah, unfortunately at this stage we would only endanger ourselves. We would have to cross lines of attack only for a fraction of a moment, and we would both be dead. I have trained you as no other man has been trained. Greatness lies on the morrow. You are not some tin soldier to go marching off to his death because bugles call. You are what you are, and what you are does not march foolishly to his death. No training, no skill, no energy or force can overcome the mind of a fool. Do not be a fool. This I command.'

'I cannot obey that command, little father.'

Chiun spun to face his television set, and turning it on, he remained silent.

Remo changed to a loose-fitting suit. The wound had caked and was becoming itchy. He ignored it. At the door to the suite, Remo said good-bye to the Master of Sinanju.

'Thank you, little father, for what you have given me.'

Without turning to set his eyes upon Remo, Chiun spoke.

'You have a chance. He may not conceive that a white man can do what you do.'

'Then I do have a chance. Why are you so glum?'

'Chances are for cards and dice. Not for us. My teaching is like the rose fragrance in a north wind.'

'Will you wish me luck?'

'You have learned naught,' said Chiun, and was silent again.

SIXTEEN

The traffic jam into Nuihc Street stretched for miles. Remo got out of the taxi and trotted past the cars with angry frustrated drivers, men who had been told in the wee hours of the morning that the final day of the convention was to be in a new building, the new headquarters of the International Brotherhood of Drivers.

When a few had complained that they already had a headquarters in Washington, they were told that Washington would be only the drivers' headquarters. Confusing. There were lots of confusing things about their new president. This was one more.

Remo pushed his way through a long line of men at the entrance, weaving and dodging complaints of 'Hey, don't you know how to get in line?'

A few recognized him as the new recording secretary. The guard at the gate was wearing a bandage. Oh, that was the man who had held his fish last night, at the beginning of the long night in which every effort to avoid the extreme plan had failed—and ultimately the extreme plan itself had failed.

The guard did not recognize him in daylight. He looked at Remo's delegate card.

'Oh yeah,' said the guard. 'Jethro wants to see you. He's right inside.'

Remo saw Jethro in the large entrance hallway. Drapes hid what was obviously a sign. Perhaps those drapes would unveil the driver's emblem, or worse, the emblem of the new superunion.

Jethro greeted people as they arrived with the usual 'howarya,' and 'goodtoseeya.' Remo walked up to within a spit. He saw Jethro notice him, saw the faint flicker of fear in the blue eyes, then the phony smile.

'Howarya fella, good to see ya,' said the president of the International Brotherhood of Drivers.

'Glad to be here, Gene. A great day. A great day,' said the recording secretary. They embraced warmly, the drivers lined up watching union solidarity at work.

'Let's go downstairs. I want to talk to you. Union business.'

'Good idea,' said Remo.

Friendly, the two union leaders made their way to the elevator. Friendly, they got into the elevator. Friendly, they spoke until the doors closed and Jethro had pressed the combination button.

'You lying sonuvabitch,' said Jethro. 'You said you had joined us.'

'You're hurt that I lied,' laughed Remo. 'When were you born?'

'Who do you work for?' said Jethro.

'I don't work for Nuihc,' said Remo. 'Where is he?'

'None of your business,' said Jethro.

'Am I going to meet him?'

'Sure,' said Jethro, a cold smile crossing his face.

Remo hummed. He hummed as they entered the large basement. He hummed as he saw the auto-length sign for the union that would destroy a nation and the union movement with it. He hummed as Jethro worked the combination lock on a door to a room that seemed the center of a whole waterpipe network.

He hummed when the door shut behind him.

Jethro went behind a barren iron desk. Remo spotted the nozzles on the ceiling, shower nozzles.

Jethro reached under the desk.

'I have a switch here that will unleash something that will kill you painfully. Now I can make it hard on you, or I can kill you with my hands.'

Remo shouldn't have done it. It was highly unprofessional. But the laugh was out before he thought of controlling it.

'Sorry,' said Remo. 'I just thought of a joke.'

'All right. Have it your way,' said Jethro. 'I can stop this process when it becomes very painful and then you'll beg me to let you talk.'

'Right,' said Remo fighting back an instant guffaw. 'Beg. Right. Beg you.' But it was no use. He laughed, and then let the laughter roar out full and pleasing.

He stopped laughing when a fine spray began forming from the nozzles. Jethro donned a mask. Obviously the substance was to be breathed in. Let your blood stream carry the poison, and perhaps, if it followed an old, simple mechanism of Sinanju discarded in the twelfth century, perhaps Remo would begin to dissolve.

The masters of Sinanju discarded this mechanism because someone accidentally discovered a simple defense to it. Don't breathe. Practically any swimmer could overcome it, and everyone who had body discipline thought it a joke. Besides, the whole machinery was cumbersome and the children liked to play with it, so, as Chiun had said, it went the way of the bow and arrow.

Remo watched Jethro stare at him sardonically through the eyes of the oxygen mask. Remo suddenly noticed one danger. Laughter. He turned his eyes away from Jethro and tried to think of something sad. He couldn't. So he thought of Dr. Smith and all the discomforting things of his life. In a few moments, the fog began to disappear into an exhaust system. Jethro ripped off his oxygen mask. A look of triumphant hate was on his face.

'Die,' he said. 'Die painfully because you now cannot move your hands or your mouth or your eyes. You can barely hear me now. So let me tell you before the hearing goes, you are going to dissolve into a puddle. A puddle like people step into. A puddle that will flush along with the rest of the scum into the sewer system.'

Too much. Dr. Smith and every sad thing in his life

could not overcome this.

'Yahhhh,' said Remo curling over and grabbing his sides in hysterical laughter. The roaring, guffawing laughter made him stagger to a wall for balance. He looked back at Jethro. There was shock. The shocked face of Jethro. It was hysterical. Why didn't Jethro stop doing those hysterical things? Perhaps Jethro thought it was the mist that was affecting him. Remo regained control.

'Sorry,' said Remo. 'Sorry to laugh at you. Where's Nuihc.'

'Uh,' said Jethro.

'Nuihc,' said Remo.

'First door to your right. Knock three times.'

Jethro's mouth hung open. Beads of sweat formed on his head. He rubbed his hands on his bell bottom suit. Then anger. He assumed his stance. Remo peered around the desk at the toes. They were pressed too far in. A beginner's mistake.

'The toes,' said Remo. 'Too far in.'

'Come and get it,' said Jethro.

Remo reached a hand around the desk and felt for the socket. Jethro tried to crack the hand with a downstroke. Remo merely removed Jethro's hand. At the wrist.

When he saw the mist coming from the nozzle, Remo ripped the mask and the tubing from its desk connection.

Jethro's one hand gripped the bloody stump of his other hand. Remo took a large green Garby Bag from a shelf. Obviously the mist did not affect plastic. He slipped the bag under Jethro and sat him down on the desk. Like putting pants on a baby, Remo slipped the bag up to Jehhro's armpits. Jethro's eyes widened in terror. His face reddened from trying not to breathe. Remo got a little metal twister that came with the Garby's and poked it into Jethro's solar plexus to help him breathe. He did. Exhale, then, full inhale.

'Don't lose the twist,' said Remo. 'Some of these bags can open by themselves if you don't have the twist.'

Then, he walked out, shutting the door behind him and breathing clean full basement air. Which was not the best of air in the world, but it would not kill him.

The first door on the right. Remo saw it immediately. He had one edge, which he had never mentioned to Chiun. Having been trained in Sinanju, Nuihc would be vulnerable to this edge. Chiun had grown to expect certain levels of performance from Remo. But Nuihc would not expect white hands to move that fast. Not expect a white body to respond that well. Not expect Remo to be what he was. Nuihc would be vulnerable to the constant danger to which every student and master of Sinanju was vulnerable. The constant danger they were taught to avoid from birth. Overconfidence. They were taught this constantly precisely because they were vulnerable.

Remo knocked three times.

'Come in, Remo,' sounded a thin voice.

Remo opened the door into a room that was a garden. There, sitting beside a pool, was Nuihc, his face that of a young Chiun, smooth and alive, and just a mite deadlier than Chiun.

Remo pretended not to see the body in its surroundings, pretended he did not have the eyes that could see things meant to be hidden.

'Over here. By the pool,' said Nuihc.

'I don't see you. Oh, yeah. There you are,' said Remo.

'Yes. Over here. Where you saw me the first time, Remo. Anyone who can work the Scarlet Ribbon, can see a man sitting peacefully.'

Remo closed the door behind him.

'Come. Sit by me.'

Remo stood still. He would have more room to analyze the attack with some distance between them.

Nuihc smiled. 'Very bright. Good. I like that. Did you kill Jethro? Of course you did. You wouldn't be here if you hadn't. You probably think me foolish in giving you the knowledge that I knew you saw me. As our mutual teacher has often taught, we should give nothing. But I give you something because I want something in return. Chiun has obviously done a remarkable job.' Remo picked up a note of condescension in the voice. Nuihc had just given too much.

'Yeah,' said Remo. 'I'm pretty good.' Maybe Nuihc would take just a mite more. Accept the boast as a sign of weakness and stupidity.

'Come, come, Remo. Let us not indulge in such silliness. Let us indulge in what you are and what you want. What do you want?'

'I want to kill you.'

'Ah, do not try to throw me off with such foolishness. We do not have time. I saw you on television the other day. Magnificent. You spoke well. You loved it. You made very pretty songs. Chiun has told you what we mean by songs, I presume.'

'Yes,' said Remo.

'Good. We need a new president of the International Brotherhood of Drivers who will become president of a new transportation union. I presume that is why you are here. To stop it. Of course you are. Remo, your presidency is only your first step to power. Come with me and all men will be at your feet. All crowds will listen to your voice. All men will proclaim you great. Your name. Your being. You will be known far and wide. Come, join.'

'I'd have to leave the persons I work for. I have a strong commitment to them.'

'Really. I don't know whom you work for, but I wonder what they have done for you. Tell me. Honestly. What have they done for you?'

'I get whatever I need.'

'Really. What? Maybe I can stop it. Seriously, what do you get?'

'Well, I have just about all the money I need.'

'And that buys you?'

'Uh, clothes, food, although I imagine you know the diet I'm on, it's necessary.'

'That you would have to undergo, with me or them.

Yes, what else?'

'Uh, I don't have to worry about rent.'

'Hmmm. You have several palaces, I take it.'

'Well, no. You see I live mostly in hotels here and there.'

'Oh, I see. Yes, I know now how they have you. You're a tool.'

'No. No. It's I can do pretty much what I want.'

'What do you want to do? You know that games of physical skill are of no interest to us. The challenge is too little. What do you do?'

'Train mostly.'

'A good tool needs that. What do you really want, Remo? Come on. We're being honest. I'll tell you whatever you want to know about me. Tell you how I cheated my village. Tell you even what makes me unhappy or happy. Come on. We're graduates of that same school.'

'All right, Nuihc. I want a home. I mean a home. And I want a family, not those one-night stands where it's more work in the line of business than it is love. I'd like to screw a woman once just to get off my rocks, not to get into her mind. I'd like to yell at a kid. My kid. And hold my kid. And teach my kid not to be afraid.'

'The president of the new transportation union will be required to have a wife and family.'

'Yeah, and I'll be dead in a year.'

'With both of us working together?'

'I don't want to have to kill Chiun.'

'He wouldn't come against both of us, Remo.'

Remo waited a minute, staring vacantly at the floor.

'Done,' he said. 'I've got to do something for myself for once.' He opened his hand and offered it to Nuihc. He walked openly to him, with the sign that he bore no weapon. Nuihc smiled broadly and extended his hand, too.

'The greater union is us. You and me,' said Nuihc.

The hands met, but Remo's kept going, slicing into the padded shoulder of the suit, taking bone in the first exhilarating feeling of a score in attack. He had scored against this Nuihc, and so well and so thoroughly that he moved into an interior line attack for the kill. No waiting to work up the shoulder and safely take it apart for the more cautious attack. With the incredible speed and force of the perfect blow, Remo brought the elbow into the chest. But the chest was not there. Mistake. Remo had scored because of over-confidence and trust on the other side, and now he would die for the same reason. His elbow was forward in air, and he was off balance because the blow needed a body to meet it.

A searing pain ripped his ribs and tore from his ribs to his shoulder. He was going dully forward, down onto a pathway of rocks. He could not move. He was not dead, but he could not move. He felt his mouth fill with warm wetness. Blood. He saw it spill onto the rock path, form a little stream, and then tip over into the clear, blue pool, making it foggy where it landed.

'Fool,' said Nuihc. 'Fool. Why are you such a fool? Magnificent you were. That was magnificent. In ten years you could have killed me. In ten years your interior attack would have worked also. But you are a fool. Fool. Fool. Together we could rule the world. Together all would be yours. But you attacked me, fool. And you attacked like a fool.'

Remo tried to see Nuihc for the final blow he knew would come shortly. But he could not move his head. He could only stare at the growing foggy area where the water, now filling with his life, had once been clear.

Then a voice, a voice Remo knew well.

'You talk of fools, Nuihc. You are the fool of fools. Did you think my student would desert his village as you have deserted yours. Did you think the Master of Sinanju would desert a student as you have deserted your blessed village of Sinanju.' Chiun's voice was filled with anger.

'Master. This is a white man. You would not harm me for a white man, me a son of the village of Sinanju.'

'For this white man, as you call him, I would rent the

core of the earth and fill its molten center with the blood of a thousand such as you. Beware. If this white man, as you call him, is dying, I shall take your ears and make you chew them, you dog-dropping.'

'But you cannot turn your skills on a member of your village, even a member who has deserted,' said Nuihc.

'Duck-hearted one, dare you speak the rules of the Master of Sinanju, your infamy still trailing behind you like excrement in the wind. Speak you now to me of the rules?'

'He is not dead and will not die.' Nuihc's voice trembled with fear.

Strange, thought Remo, he should not fear. He should have been trained to deal with fear because next to arrogance, fear was the major enemy. Stranger still was Chiun's boast to Nuihc, and the insults. Chiun had always said to threaten damage was to give a man a shield. To spew insults was to give him energy, except in a case where the enemy could be provoked to foolish anger. From his voice, Nuihc was obviously not angry. It must be, thought Remo, that Chiun knew Nuihc could not be fooled by talk of peace or appearances of weakness.

'Leave,' said Chiun.

'I leave, but I have ten years in which to deprive you of your special student.'

'Why do you let me know this?'

'Because I hate you and your father and your direct lineage from the original Master of Sinanju.'

Remo heard faint footsteps scurry out to the hall. He tried to call out to Chiun to stop him, but even if he could, he wondered whether Chiun would try. He felt Chiun's hands on his back working quickly and deftly, and suddenly the incredible, immobilizing pain filtered away and Remo could move his head, then his shoulders, and with great pain begin to sit up slowly.

'Now you can move,' said Chiun.

With a sudden wrenching of his back, Remo sat up, grimacing. He tried to control it. He did not wish the little father see him succumb to pain.

'Rush. Rush,' said Chiun angrily. 'You are so American. You could not wait a measly five years.'

'I had to do my job.'

'Do not make that mistake again, but I respected you for it. Next time you will be ready for Nuihc. I cannot kill another member of the village.'

'But I heard you say you would.'

'You hear many foolish things. Quiet your insolent tongue. He has made a grave mistake. It is not ten years. And that sort of mistake at our level is deadly.'

'What if he returns in less than five years?'

'We run. Time is on our side. Why give away advantages?'

'Yes, little father.'

Something still troubled Remo.

'Did you really mean I would be better than the Masters of Sinanju eventually, even though I am not Korean.'

'No,' said Chiun. 'That was a song for your benefit.'

'I do not believe you,' said Remo.

'Silence! You have almost destroyed in one foolish moment my work of years.'

Remo was silent. Then he lifted himself to his feet, wincing.

'Good,' said Chiun. 'Pain is an excellent teacher. What your mind cannot grasp, your body will never forget. Remember this in your pain. Never rush. Time is your ally or your enemy.'

'There are some things I must do now, little father.'

'Well, be quick about it. A shirt is not the best bandage in the world, even a shirt tied by me.'

SEVENTEEN

Remo mounted the podium in the large hall of the new building. Wild, hysterical cheering met his ascent. He waved his good arm to quiet the crowd. But the roar continued and he met it with a smile for the television cameras, the still photographers and, last but not least, his audience.

A new shirt covered his torso, and the jacket was so arranged as to hide the knots Chiun had installed. The pain continued sharp and throbbing, but Remo smiled. He smiled at the three union presidents sitting on the speaker's platform. He smiled at the secretary of labor and he smiled at the delegates he knew. Especially at Abe 'Crowbar' Bludner, who appeared to be cheering the loudest.

The hall in this new building was smaller than Convention Hall, but is was roomy enough for the driver delegates. There were even some empty seats in the second balcony.

Remo leaned down into the mike. The noise subsided.

'Brother drivers,' he said. 'Brother drivers. I have sad news that will come as a shock to you.' Remo paused to allow the hall to become still, to glean the last bit of attention from the audience. He looked at the few key men he had called to him just an hour ago. They knew what the shock would be. Gene Jethro, always a kook, had run out on the union. Remo had explained this to the few delegates an hour before. His explanation had been believed instantly, because there was no reason for not believing it. Remo had spoken to those key men in a small receptionist's room while most of the membership was still filing into the hall.

They had less than an hour to decide among themselves what the union would do. There were less than a dozen men in the small office.

'You can let this go to the vice-president of the international, or you can make yourself a good deal now. You know the vice-president was only chosen to balance the ticket.'

The key delegates nodded. Some sat on chairs, two leaned against a desk, one of them sat on the large pot holding a palm tree. There were sounds of approval. This kid knew what he was doing.

Remo continued. 'If we choose the new president now, we can stampede the convention. If we have somebody, nobody can beat us. All we have to do is come to an agreement now. It's gonna be our union or it's gonna be chaos. It's up to you guys to decide. Jethro is gone. You want to make a president now among us?'

In the confusion of the sudden announcement, one delegate offered the job to Remo.

Remo shook his head. 'I know someone better. I know someone perfect,' Remo had said.

That was an hour ago, and now as he faced the full membership, he knew he could stampede the entire convention momentarily. Remo looked out over the faces of the silent delegates, tobacco smoke rising blue to the ceiling.

'The sad news is that our president, Gene Jethro, has left. He has resigned and left the country. He left giving me this note.' Remo waved a paper out in front of the podium. It was blank. But only he could see that.

'I'm not going to read you the words, because the words don't convey Gene Jethro's love of the Brotherhood of Drivers, of unionism, and the American way of life. The words aren't good enough. It was his heart that counted. And what was in his heart was love for you. He told me he thought he wasn't old enough to be president. Yes. That's what he told me. I told him age was measured in more than years. It is measured in honesty and courage and in love for our union. I told him he had an abundance of that, but he would not listen. He said he had won the election but was afraid to lead. He said he was going off to a place he knew where he could think. This resignation says all that. But I don't need it to tell you what was in his heart.'

Remo tore the blank paper into tiny strips, and the tiny strips into confetti.

The convention was mumbling now. Many of the delegates were shocked. But certain key delegates were not shocked. They were ready and had been for an hour. They waited for Remo to complete the deal they had made.

'We cannot be leaderless in the troubled sea of trade unionism. We cannot run without rudder or keel,' Remo intoned. 'We have a man who has worked his way up union ranks. A man who stands with the drivers, behind the drivers and in the forefront of the drivers, lo these many years. A man who knows strength yet is strong with charity. A man who knows unionism as well as peopleism. A man who has led and has followed. A man who has been a driver stalwart in the dark hours of defeat and in the sunny hours of victory. There is only one man this union can elect as president to replace our beloved Gene Jethro. That man is my own local president from New York City, Abraham Bludner.'

At the sound of the name, the key delegates led their followers into the aisles for a spontaneous demonstration. Their numbers swelled as each delegate saw the center of new power and did not want to be reminded at some crucial time during the next four years that he had sat on his ass when Abe Bludner needed him most.

Remo waved at Bludner who was now being carried to the podium on the shoulders of his men. Bludner had been ready for this even before the key delegates had been asked to the special caucus meeting. Remo, the politician, had stampeded the fewer than dozen men the way he would stampede the entire convention. He had met with Bludner in Nuihc's private rooms, fountain and all. Bludner had given it a suspicious look, so Remo had shrugged, indicating that he, too, thought it odd.

'Abe,' said Remo, sitting by the pool where he had almost lost his life. 'How would you like to be president of the International Brotherhood of Drivers?'

'In four years I'll be too old, kid.'

'I'm talking about this afternoon.'

'What about Jethro?'

'Jethro has had a little family trouble. He's out of the picture for good.'

'Oh,' said Bludner. 'One of those things.'

'One of those things,' said Remo.

'What do you want?' asked Bludner.

'A few favors.'

'Of course, what?'

'You don't know whom I represent. But let's not go into that. It is of little import. There are some other allied unions, other transportation unions that want to merge with us. They plan to announce it today. That was Jethro's plan. People who have plans like that tend to have unfortunate family problems also, if you know what I mean?'

Bludner knew what Remo meant.

'I don't think the drivers should ever merge with another union. Do you?'

'And lose our independence? said Bludner indignantly.

'From time to time the organization I work for needs information on who is doing what. They won't hurt your union. Of course, you will be paid for the favor of supplying information.'

Bludner thought about that. He nodded.

'You will be contacted by someone. Do not mention me. You never knew me. Right?'

'You leaving?'

'You want to be president, Abe?'

'Kid, I used to think about it, but when I became, I think around 45, I stopped. You know. It was a dream then and it went with all the other dreams. I wouldn't run the international the way I run the local. I think we could do with a bit more class in the international.' Bludner smiled. 'Of course, not so much class that I'll be a one-term president.'

'Now who are the key delegates?' Remo had asked, and Bludner had told him. He also told him they couldn't meet them privately in the room 'with the flowers and everything, 'cause they'll think we're a little bit, you know, kid.'

Remo knew. The delegates went for Bludner in private the way they were going for him now in the open convention. The vice-president would be no trouble, Remo had assured them. He was, after all, a lightweight, as everyone agreed, and he would forgo the legal succession. There would be a court case, of course, from some dissidents, but it could be dragged out in the courts until Bludner solidified his power nationally, as he had learned to do locally years before.

Remo had picked a good man. He watched a handful of delegates struggle up the platform steps with Bludner on their shoulders. Bludner tapped a few heads, indicating that he wished to walk up by himself. When he got to the podium, there was a roar. Remo hugged Abe. Abe hugged Remo.

Smiling at the crowd, Remo said out of the corner of his mouth, so that only Bludner could hear:

'You live as long as you keep the deal, Abe.'

'I understand, kid,' said Bludner.

Remo glanced over his shoulder at the presidents of the three other transportation unions. They, too, were reasonable men, although one of them sat very carefully on a very painful spinal column.

When the enthusiasm was surmountable, Remo yelled

into the microphone.

'Voice vote. All in favor of Abe Bludner as president, say "Aye."'

The hall exploded in a roar of ayes.

'All against, say "Nay."'

There was a single 'nay' that was met by laughter.

'Carried. The new president is Abe Bludner.'

There was more cheering and more hysteria.

Remo quieted the audience. 'Before I introduce my good and long-time friend, Abe Bludner, to the union he now leads, I would like to say a few words.'

Remo looked out into the balcony. A few driver wives dotted those seats. He thought of Chris at the airport. She would wait and he would never come. She would be met instead by agents of the FBI who had a tip. Her testimony would end the careers of the presidents of the three other unions. That exposure, including their using of union funds to pay for the construction of a building for another union, would end their careers for all time. It would also kill the merger idea. The superunion was dead. In a few days at most, Remo Jones would cease to exist. There would be a new face and maybe even a new regional accent. He would never have that family or home, any more than he could now eat a hamburger laced with monosodium glutamate. So be it. He was what he was, and all the longing in the world could not change that.

'I want to tell you something I mean very much,' said Remo. His voice was steady, free of the orator's rising pitches. 'You have heard many things about America and its wealth. You have heard about its coming demise. You have heard many people say we are rich and fat and weak. But I ask you, where did that wealth come from?

'Did someone give it to you? Did you find it on the streets? Did your parents or grandparents find it on the street? No, I say to you, you are the wealth of this nation. You are what makes it strong. Other continents have more raw material and they are impoverished. Look at

South America. Look at Africa. Look at most of Asia and look at many sections of Europe. No, the wealth of any nation is its people, the willingness of its people to work and to get for themselves and their families the best things they can.

'This country is not strong because of some mineral deposit somewhere. Other countries have more and are weak and backward. This country is strong because it offers hope. And strong people have taken that hope. You represent drivers. They are part of that hope. That hope lives. And I say to you, very honestly, it is an honor to die for it.'

The last sentence seemed overdramatic to many delegates, even though dramatics was the way with many of these convention speeches. What they could not realize was that they had not heard a song.

A few delegates believed they saw tears in the eyes of their new recording secretary that day. A few said that when he left the building just outside Chicago, he was crying openly. None of them saw him again.

THE END

THE DESTROYER: DEATH CHECK
by RICHARD SAPIR and WARREN MURPHY

The Brewster Forum—a collection of the world's top scientists involved in super-cerebral research projects. One of their more interesting secret studies is the drafting of a plan to control the world. A federal security agent is murdered and unless the murderer can be found and destroyed soon, the Brewster Forum may have to be eliminated along with its vital secrets. Only one force could handle the assignment—CURE, and its unique human weapon—Remo Williams . . .

THE DESTROYER

0 552 09405 6—**30p** **T45**

THE DESTROYER: CHINESE PUZZLE
by RICHARD SAPIR and WARREN MURPHY

The Chinese Premier has agreed to a state visit to the U.S.A. His first emissary is poisoned aboard an aircraft—along with the rest of the passengers. A second emissary despatched following a secret route known only to the Chinese, is kidnapped from his car, his driver and aide murdered. Peace between East and West is finally within reach and America's security forces have failed . . .

In the White House the President reaches for the special phone which he has used only once in his career—the direct line to CURE, and its very special agent—Remo Williams . . .

THE DESTROYER

0 552 09406 4—**30p** **T46**